The Ivory Pin

Lela E. Buis

The Ivory Pin

That Ridge ~ Knoxville

The Ivory Pin

ISBN 978-0-9850190-5-1 Print
ISBN 978-0-9850190-6-8 E-book

Published by That Ridge Publishing, Knoxville TN

First Edition 2021
Printed in the United States of America

DEDICATION

For C. .J. Cherryh, always an inspiration.

"If you think you are too small to make a difference, try sleeping with a mosquito."
— *The Dalai Lama*

Table of Contents

Chapter 1

It took Da Hanath a long time to die. His screams tore through half the night, and now that it was over, Ta Nyahl hung slack and exhausted from the iron spike above his head while the ghostly firelight danced through the shadows. He knew he would be next.

He waited without any strength left, lying against the rough wooden stake. It was a hewn post with splinters sharp enough to gouge his cheek, set in the dirt at the center of the humans' village for rites of torture. He thought they used it as often as they could. These people had no mercy for their enemies—or for their own kin either—if they could catch someone in the wrong. They had murdered the last of Ta Nyahl's own clan, and tonight they would finish him off, too. It seemed vaguely ironic, as if there had been a death sentence on him ever since his kin died—only deferred for a little while.

It wouldn't take him nearly so long to die as Da Hanath, who had been older—strong and whole. Ta Nyahl was weakened already. His whole left side ached with a deadly persistence that ran bone deep. Earlier his arms had hurt just as agonizingly, but now they were numb from lack of circulation, from the tightness of the lashings around his wrists, and the stress his weight had put on the joints and ligaments. Blood had run and darkened over the bruises on his back, and had matted into his hair where it hung down in a thick snarl. It had soaked his clothes, too, before the humans had stripped those away. Blood seemed all he could smell now, a primal metallic stink that seemed to fill up his whole world. It was his own blood mixed with Da Hanath's—and the stench of seared flesh along with it that had come from the torture. Ta Nyahl's strength seemed to have gone with his blood, and now as he waited, he felt dizzy and weak with shock, and a sheer darkness came and went. Still, however much he wanted it, he hadn't been able to achieve real unconsciousness. He'd heard every sound of torment, flinched at every cut or burn they'd inflicted on Da Hanath, as if all the torture had been happening to him. And now he'd have to go through it again, but a lot more intimately this time. It was his own torment and death that he had to endure now.

Still, worse than the prospect of torture was the certainty that this was his fault, this shameful death for both of them. He writhed inwardly with the knowledge—knowing in his heart he had been damned for his desire for revenge, regardless of what he paid now. He had brought this on himself and on Da Hanath through his own stubborn anger, and only a slightly better death for Da Kathan, who had died earlier in the woods. That reality cut him worse than any knife would. So it was more than the wound in his shoulder that had left him cowering against the stake, dreading to face his predecessors with that terrible mark of shame on him.

He'd be dead already to his own people if they knew. They were as terrible in their own way as the people of this village. They were too few, and such costly mistakes of wrongful thinking couldn't be forgiven of a kria. All he could do to make amends was to remove himself from the scene as quickly as possible, to hurry after Da Hanath and Da Kathan on their final journey to the afterworld and try to find forgiveness there. He didn't have to worry about how to do it. The humans were going to handle the job for him. It was fitting punishment, too, that he should go last—but that hadn't done anything yet to reduce his guilt.

At the neighboring stake they were cutting down the bleeding remains of flesh and bone for whatever they would do with it later. Some in his village had said that men ate kria flesh. He heard the humans' laughter and obscenities dimly through the throbbing numbness of pain, along with the passing of some drink. There were women and children in the crowd, too, a state of things that only seemed to make the torture more hideous to him. It was a horror that children learned cruelty so early from their elders.

Their words flowed over him, barely understood. They were talking about the strong magic of their shaman, and how he had brought them a bounty in the capture of the kria. He wondered at their idea of magic—his people hardly believed in it, but perhaps the humans had more understanding of it than the kria.

They were ready for him now. He had faded a little, came back with a jolt as one of them caught a hand in his hair and jerked his head backward. His muscles responded automatically, and he gasped at the sudden pain of the movement. The man laughed then and hit him in the face, adding another bruise to others already there, then let go of him. They had what they wanted, knowledge that he was aware and ready to suffer.

He didn't have any resistance left, only the hope that things would go quickly. When the first glowing iron burnt his side, he flinched against the stake and screamed painfully as Da Hanath hadn't until well into the torture. His reaction only made them laugh the louder. More distant to his fading senses, they seemed to renew their celebrations.

It seemed endless. When the darkness came over him, they waited, and his whole universe was nothing but pain. Waves of agony rolled over him. He fell into a raw, mindless state where his quivering flesh only responded, jerking painfully at the bonds with each additional hurt, and his voice broke with the screaming.

But then, oddly, it seemed to stop.

He had fallen into the darkness, came back dimly. He heard voices—floated for a while, hearing and not hearing. He was helpless, and the fire in his body flickered, rising and falling with the real firelight. He forgot everything but that agony—even that he wanted to die.

It was an argument he heard, human voices. A woman's, he thought in a brief second of lucidity. It seemed authoritative and raised in anger. That meant nothing to him at first, and then something, too, as it had to be what was responsible for this pause. She was complaining about the noise, he thought.

Realization only touched him for a second; then he was gone again. As a result he was only vaguely aware of a shadow next to him, and he failed to realize what was happening. The thong that had bound his hands to the ring above him parted suddenly and he fell. He skinned his shoulder and the side of his face on the rough splinters of the stake, but he was hardly aware of it. Someone kicked him roughly, and he fought back to the surface, gasping for breath as if he were drowning, trying to focus. The argument was going on closer to him now.

"You owe me, headman," the woman was saying, "for the life of your son." Her voice was lower now, but still demanding.

"Not this," the man's voice answered her. "Ask for something else, woman."

The two shadows stood at a little distance, silhouetted against the fire. The others, drawn further back, shuffled and murmured. He became aware of tension, the scent of fear and anger almost palpable around him. It washed over him like cold water, nearly cleared his mind.

"I need a servant," the woman said. "And here's one available. You'll give me what I want, or I'll take it."

She sounded cold and forbidding even to Ta Nyahl, lying half-conscious in the dirt. This time he heard the murmur that ran through the crowd. "Witch," they said. The word didn't mean a lot to him, distant as he was.

But then hands took hold of him, jerked him up. They meant for him to kneel at her feet, but when they thrust him down he fell on his face, unable to use his bound hands even to catch himself.

"You want this?" the man hissed, and his derision was clear. "This thing will never serve you."

"Wait," she said. She made some gesture warning the man off. A shadow blocked the firelight completely then, and Ta Nyahl felt her close in on him. She had him by the shoulder before he'd realized her intention. Half-dazed as he was, still he tried to flinch away from her, and she dug her nails in, sharp as claws.

"Are you awake?" she asked him. "Can you hear me?"

He wasn't able to answer, but she must have known he was awake from the way he had moved. She shook him, and it hurt, as if it rattled his very bones.

"I want you to listen," she said, tense and quiet above his ear. She seemed to be speaking just to him. "I need someone to serve me. But I won't take on someone who's hostile or who will run off at the first opportunity."

The words slid by him. Only a thread of meaning caught anywhere in the broken shards of his intelligence. She shook him again.

"Do you hear me?" she asked. "I'll actually take the fact that you're here in this situation as a recommendation."

That seemed a strange thing to say, and he began to struggle with her language and intent then, trying to follow what she was asking of him. She had mistaken him for a human, he decided, and she wanted to take him as a slave according to their custom. He shuddered at the idea, outraged, though he wouldn't have thought he was capable.

"No," he whispered. It was only a breath through cut and swollen lips, and it made her angry. Her nails dug into his shoulder again.

"Dammit, I'm trying to help you," she hissed. "Swear to me you'll do it." She waited then, but he kept his mouth shut, locating the dregs of rightness somewhere, even in this delirium. He had meant to die, and then ask forgiveness of his predecessors.

"If you won't," she said then, "I'll damn sure take you anyway, and just get rid of you somewhere else. Do you hear me? I'm not going to spend the rest of the night listening to you die."

It went too fast, and he didn't understand her. He was disoriented again, lost and groping after a logic he hadn't any hope of understanding. But she didn't wait for him. She only shifted to another attack.

"What do you want?" she demanded. "Your friend's body?" Her nails bit at him. "Whatever you need—I've just got to stop this somehow. Swear you'll serve me."

It was a masterful stroke, and he vaguely knew he was defeated. She had trapped him finally and irrevocably. Da Hanath's dignity even in death meant more to him than his own life. If he could win that back, he would, even at the cost of his own salvation.

The woman's breath hissed out at his continued silence, and now her hand loosened. She moved as if she meant to leave him. Quickly, before she could go, he said it, to call her back.

"What?" she said, as if it had been too muffled by pain and sickness for her to hear.

"I swear," he whispered again in the human language, fighting to make it clearer. He felt her tense slightly, as if she had really believed what the human man had said, that he would never do it. This seemed a fitting punishment for him. He had always hated the humans, and now he would be obligated to one. "Please..." he said then, meaning to remind her about Da Hanath. His voice failed, nearly gone.

She seemed not to hear it, pushed away from him and rose.

"What did he say?" the man asked her.

"Yes," the woman said simply. But she had understood that last plea after all. "This is what I want," she said. "Both of them, and gear for this one. Give them to me along with the horses you've already supplied, and you've discharged your debt."

The headman's breath gusted out in scorn, and Ta Nyahl heard the rustle of angry whispers through the crowd.

"Take them," the headman said, sounding half choked.

They must be anxious to be rid of the woman, whatever the reasons.

In another moment she knelt again and tugged at Ta Nyahl's hands. He didn't move, couldn't resist, lay completely limp in his defeat. She unsheathed a knife and searched out a place where the bindings weren't sunk completely into the flesh of his wrists. She cut the leather and peeled it away, but in his numbness he couldn't feel any difference. She rubbed at the scored flesh until sharp new pains started in his fingers from the returning circulation. He winced, and then she pushed away and stood.

"Get up," she said to him, sounding cold. "Or do you need help?"

Half-dazed, still he realized what that would mean. He didn't want the humans to touch him again, so he gathered himself and made the effort, staggered to his feet. She reached to steady him as he reeled, but he caught his balance and rocked back, evading her.

"All right then," she said, dropping her hands. "Follow me."

She set off through the dying firelight and he followed, sick and uncertain, fighting dizziness, with a final glance behind. The humans seemed ready to do as she said. They were circled, watching spitefully, but standing well away from Da Hanath's body, as if she had cursed it somehow. For the moment it was enough.

Ta Nyahl could have run away. Probably he could have evaded them in the darkness, even hurt and disoriented as he was. But he was trapped in a way that left him desperate and frightened. Honor meant a great deal to the kria. He had sworn, and so he stumbled after her. She seemed not to be staying in the village. In a moment they arrived at a sentry's shelter a little distance beyond the palisade. She ducked inside the hut of mud and sticks, and he waited by the fire embers, wavering on his feet, wondering what he was supposed to do. He started to sit down, or maybe to fall over, but then she reappeared.

"There's a spring over there," she said, pointing, "and this is soap. Go wash." She held something out to him.

She had seen the blood then, and the filth and dirt that clung to it, was fastidious enough not to want it around her. He took what she gave him, without touching her fingers, and went searching. He found the pool easily enough from the sounds of the steam, and slid into it carefully, expecting that the cold water would hurt. It did. It made the bruises ache and left him shivering painfully, but then, too, it cooled the sting of his burns. Leaning his head down against the rocks for a while helped the dizziness. He didn't like the smell of the soap and didn't know what it was for, so he left it on the bank and scrubbed with sand instead, as he usually did. His teeth were chattering violently before he had soaked the blood out of his hair. He climbed up out of the water thinking he would die of the cold before he dried without any sun to hurry the process, but the woman had left him a blanket. He wiped the water off himself with his hands, going carefully past the wounds, and wrung out his hair, wrapped the rough wool around him. The cleanliness and warmth were scant comforts, but after he had rested a while, he pushed up again and found his way back.

The woman was waiting for him at the shelter nervously, as if she wasn't sure her commands would be obeyed. She almost started when she saw him, as if she'd thought he wouldn't come back.

"What do you want done with your friend's body?" she asked, straight out. It sounded harsh and callous that way, and her face was cold and unfeeling—but that was no more than he could expect. He would be dishonored among his own people for causing two deaths, and he hadn't died to atone for it. His worst fears had come true, the terrors of his childhood. This night had left him outcast and alone—and he had agreed to become a human's slave. He would do well to be tolerated by a human. He didn't expect anything from this woman—but it did seem that she meant to keep her promise, anyway.

He sank down and dropped his head on his knees, unable to even address the problem of how to treat a body that was already so profaned. At least they hadn't found Da Kathan in the woods. Da Hanath had covered the body with leaves in time.

"Bury it?" she asked.

"No," he whispered.

She seemed taken aback—it was the humans' custom, after all. When he didn't offer anything else, she tried again. "Should I have it left for your kin to find?"

"Yes." He thought perhaps that would be best. His people exposed their dead after a solemn ritual, to return to the earth.

"Then I'll take care of it," she said. "Rest for a while."

Her voice seemed kinder somehow, and he felt almost grateful, less grieved as she left him, though he didn't have much trust in her. Likely he should carry the body out himself to keep the humans from touching it, but he was hardly able to stand right now, and he wasn't sure his touch would be an honor to Da Hanath anyway. Better to have strangers serve him than a kinsman who was dishonored—as long as it was truly done as the woman said. And better scavengers attend to Da Hanath in the woods without the ritual preparations than a human burial, regardless of whether the kria ever knew what had happened to him. He, himself, could whisper the prayers, for whatever good they would do.

The question of propriety wasn't something he could consider for very long. He ached with a bone-deep exhaustion that made everything seem remote, even fear for his soul. Ta Nyahl didn't like the smell of the shelter. He searched out a place in the brush to collapse, and let unconsciousness fall on him like a stone.

Chapter 2

Full daylight lightened his sleep. A leaf rustled near him and he lurched awake, jerked up. He had chosen his cover with automatic instincts, rocks to give him protection against arrow flight, brush for a screen. Pain and dizziness came down on him together, and he fell back hard against the stone. He lay there panting, his face against the cold rock, his terror fading only slightly as memory returned. The sound was only the woman who owned him and not one of the other villagers—still it was waking to a nightmare. She must have searched him out in the brush, not having found him in the shelter, and she stood there for a moment studying him. Then she knelt suddenly, caught the mass of his hair in one hand and thrust it back away from his face.

In darkness and filth and shifting firelight it was understandable she could mistake him for a human man. Humans and kria were surprisingly similar for two species that had met so randomly. But in full daylight and with her hands on him, there wasn't any way she could miss the difference. The basic coloring was the same, but his hair was coarse as a horse's tail, frosted just now in blue and white, and the bone structure of his face was different, more prominent than a human's. More permanent than the bruises, a blue shadow lay across the brown of his cheekbones like a mask.

He waited for her reaction, for her to jerk backward or perhaps to strike him for deceiving her. But she only took a sharper breath, and her hand trembled slightly where she held him.

"God," she said. "What are you?"

"Kria-en," he whispered, answering her through swollen lips. His face was still tight against the stone, averted. It was shameful for her to touch him this way, and to stare at him. But it was something he'd have to endure. He couldn't expect her to have any regard for either his person or his pride.

"What's your name?" she asked then, as if suddenly uncertain he would have one. Her hand shook, and she sounded as if her voice was about to fail.

He gave it.

"Ta Nyahl," she repeated, and the syllables were awkward on her tongue. It wasn't the way he'd said it, but her ear was quick. She had caught the basic sounds.

"My name is Cybelle Lawton," she said. Then her grip tightened in his hair. "Look at me."

It seemed indecent. He wanted to refuse, and the very idea injured him that he had to raise his eyes from the cool stone to face her. But this woman owned him now, by his own decision. It was his duty to obey her, so he smothered his objections finally and did it, lifted his eyes to meet hers as boldly as she looked at him.

She was younger than he expected from the authority in her voice, and taller, with skin and hair that were surprisingly light. He felt her hand twitch at sight of his vertical pupils, but she didn't let go of him. She only tightened her fingers and looked fiercer than ever. "Ta Nyahl," she said, "I didn't know what you were."

It was no surprise, but still he trembled, expecting she would reject him now, and the oath he had sworn. Maybe she would throw him back to the villagers, and thus complete his dishonor. He dropped his eyes and turned his face against the stone, and she let go of him. Perhaps she felt the pain that had come with her words.

"Please..." he whispered, as he had in the darkness, and lay there in complete misery. He wanted to keep his part of the bargain, knowing he had to pay for the ease of Da Hanath's soul.

The woman hissed out a breath, gripped her hands suddenly into fists.

"Dammit," she said. "This is a complication." Then she sat there on her heels for a while looking at him, chewing her lower lip. He didn't move, couldn't find a way to respond to her except by stillness.

"Are you all right?" she asked finally. It was a complicated question, and one he couldn't answer right away. She waited, apparently realized at last that he wouldn't reply. "I don't like this place, and I want to get out of here," she explained. "Whatever else I do with you, I will take you away with me." And then she hesitated again. "Or maybe you'll tell me what you mean to do once we're away?"

That was complicated, too, and again he didn't answer, only pressed his face tighter against the rock.

"Dammit," she said again. "They knew what you were, didn't they?" She sat there a while longer, seeming to ponder, and then she spoke to him in a lower voice. "What I said still applies, I guess—about the recommendation. I haven't got time, and I'll take a chance on you, whatever you are. If I let you rest today, can you ride a horse tonight?"

He didn't follow all she said, lost the thread of it, but that last was simpler, a matter of what he would or wouldn't do.

"Yes," he said.

He thought she sighed heavily.

"Go back to sleep then," she said. "Your friend's going to be taken care of, and I'll bring you some clothes later on. Are you hungry?"

The idea of food made his stomach turn with sickness.

"No," he said, half-choking.

"All right," she said, and forced a thin smile. It was a human expression that he thought was meant to be reassurance, but still it left him disturbed. She pushed up and stood over him, reached a hand toward his shoulder, but this time she hesitated at his cringe, seeing how he hated to be touched, and let the hand drop to her side instead. It was a kindness he hadn't expected.

He drowsed fitfully through the day, disturbed by noise now and then, or darts of pain when he moved. The woman came back at twilight and didn't startle him so completely. He had been lying on the edge of waking for a while, aware of what was happening around him and listening to the sounds of the village in the distance. They were faint, but still too close—part of the nightmare that was his life now. It would continue. There'd been nothing to limit his swearing, and after it the woman possessed him completely. He heard her boots whisk through the brush and he lay still, waiting as she stopped.

"Are you awake?" she asked. Her voice was taut and short, almost strained.

He stirred in response.

"Get dressed," she said. "I've brought you clothes. There's something for you to eat back at the shack. Then if you're able, you can do something useful and saddle the horses. I've got other things to do." She dropped a bundle of things next to him and stalked away.

The bundle consisted of the same sort of heavy clothing that she had on, the kind human warriors wore when they traveled by horse. Certainly it had come from the village. There was a coarse woolen shirt and leggings for underneath, and a jacket and split leather skirt to go over those. The jacket had peaked shoulders and laced-in sleeves, and it was plated with bone that settled over his injured shoulder with a painful weight. The boots were heavy and stiff. Ta Nyahl regretted the loss of his own clothing and the soft boots that went with it. The kria didn't wear armor, only trusted to soft doeskin and elusive ways, a natural ability to remain invisible. Still, he was stiff and sore, and with an angry, aching wound in his shoulder, he could understand the humans' liking for the heavy leather and bone, regardless of the weight.

He stood up to put it on, wavering for a moment, figuring out the order and the fastenings. They weren't so different from those his people used. The kria had come to this place unprepared to live in a forest, and they had borrowed a great deal from the humans they'd found already here—however competent and comfortable they might be in the land now. The clothes fit well enough. Someone had a good eye for size, regardless that he was lighter than a human of like stature. His shoulders were just as wide, but more flexible—this stiff clothing would cut down his usual native pliability.

Standing, he was glad to find the dizziness that had afflicted him was going. He was stiff and sore and throbbed with hurt, but it seemed bearable. He waited for a moment just breathing, and decided his strength was very fragile. Still, there was nothing he could do about it, so he picked up the blanket and followed the woman's track back to the shelter.

She was making up packs in the lee of the hut, efficiently parceling up goods to go behind the saddles, and he thought perhaps he would be riding the horse now that she would have used to carry supplies. She glanced up as he appeared, gestured toward food laid out on a cloth.

"There's not going to be anything hot," she said. "That's all I have that's cold. Hurry and eat. I don't trust that headman any further than I could throw him. He owes me hospitality, but I don't like his eyes a damn bit. I want to be gone as soon as it's full dark."

He didn't grasp half of the flow of words, but he meant to obey her. The food was bread and petrified cheese and a gourd of sour goat's milk, all of which he recognized as edible, though given a choice he would have preferred something else. He eased down to a cross-legged position and drank the milk first. Then he tried some of the bread and cheese, feeling for how it lay on his stomach—glanced up to find the woman watching him. She looked away quickly, and went back to packing as he dropped his face and let the thick curtain of his hair slide forward. Still, the glance spoiled the food for him. After he sat there a moment, he wrapped it and put it in a pocket of the leather skirt, meaning to finish it later when he had more privacy. He got up to look for the horses.

"Don't let anyone see you," the woman warned him. "I want to get out of here quietly—no fanfare."

The horses were afraid of him. There were two, a tall, rangy mare and a smallish bay gelding, hidden in the bushes a distance behind the hut. Struggling one-handed to force tack on the skittish animals, he wondered what the woman had been staring at. Likely it was the quick flash of his teeth as he bit into the hard cheese, a thing that still gave away the origins of the kria, regardless of the extent of their intelligence and civilization now. It was disturbing to humans, even when they didn't realize why they were affected. The woman wasn't immune to the effect, whatever her own people might think of her being—what had they said? A witch.

He sweated in the heavy clothes, even in the chill of early spring with night coming on fast. His hair slid into his eyes and stuck to his face as he worked, aggravating his pain. He got one of the saddles up and leaned against the unwilling horse to catch his breath, brushed the ragged ends of it back. The humans had cut away the amulet braids that usually hung before his ears and controlled the front part of its wildness. Maybe it was the loss of the charms bound in them that had exposed him to the dangers of witchcraft—if that was what he had fallen into with this woman.

Actually though, he wasn't sure that he understood the word "witch," or the differing concepts that went with it. Kria lore spoke of similar creatures called ayeen, but they were sexless demons that usually tormented a dishonored soul in the afterlife. He thought the human word "witch" only referred to a human woman who was ugly and powerful and did magical things. It seemed a vindictive term. But perhaps both were the same after all, he thought bitterly. Perhaps she was an ayeen that had come in a human's form to torment him, to make him pay for his sins. Whatever, he would have to do something about the hair as soon as he could. It was likely to blind him, flying in his face as it was.

Finished with the work, he felt ominously weak and dizzy again. He sat for a while with his head on his knees to rest while the horses twitched at their tethers and rolled their eyes at his nearness. The woman strode down the path carrying the packs and hardly glanced at him. She did look relieved to see he knew which end of a horse to put the bridle on, but again, the kria had taken horses from the humans, and although they'd made changes in the harness for convenience sake, everything he knew about it was basically human knowledge. Like the clothes, he'd had no problems in figuring it out. She checked the girths to make sure of the saddles and dropped the packs at his feet.

"Tie these on," she said. "I'm going to rig the fire to burn all night if I can, so they'll not miss us. Then we'll be gone."

He annoyed the horses again to deal with the pack bindings, but had no space to rest this time before she was back. It was full dark by then, the time she had set to move.

"That's it," she said. She threw on a cloak, all business. "Let's go. And keep it as quiet as you can."

He had trouble getting up on the mare. She resented the idea of a strange rider, kept jerking her head, shifting away from him, and he hadn't the strength to get up quickly as he needed to. Impatient, the woman grabbed the mare's head finally, and he trapped the animal against a tree, managed to pull up into the saddle.

"All right?" she asked when he was settled. When he answered her faintly, she let go, turned her horse and set off into the dark.

Chapter 3

At first he thought he wouldn't be able to do it. He'd said that he would, but the struggle to outfit the horses had sapped his strength, and now the mare's jostling gait set his wounds on fire. He didn't ask for mercy, though, only set his teeth in a fear of fainting. After a while the pain eased off to numbness as the woman settled into a steady pace on a clear trail. He vaguely doubted the wisdom of that—it wasn't something a kria would do. But it would save the horses' strength over the night's travel, so perhaps it was right after all. He didn't really understand what the woman was doing—or what it meant for anyone to be a human in the world. Because he'd always hated them so, it wasn't something he had even cared to wonder about.

It seemed strange that she had to slip away from her own kind this way. That must be what she was doing, regardless of how she went straight along the trail. It was a curious behavior to his thinking, though after a confused while, he believed he'd figured out her reasoning. The kria were small in number, and under the pressure of human enemies, the clans were close. One belonged or was an outcast, and there wasn't any bargaining with halfway positions. But humans were so numerous that they weren't all to be counted as kin.

They were cruel and hostile to one another. They abided by a bewildering contradiction of rules, too, so when they ventured outside their own clan's territory, probably they had to watch their backs or end up at some village stake as the night's entertainment. Even if the headman had owed this woman, still she must think it would pay for her to get out quietly.

It was a cynical thought that the humans might be worse enemies to their own kind than to the kria, and a new idea to him. It broadened his understanding of them, but it wasn't an immediately useful thought, so he only stored it. Then he forgot it and concentrated on staying on the horse and easing the pain of his hurts as much as he could. The night seemed to go on forever.

Ta Nyahl felt half-dead when dawn finally started to brighten the sky above the trees, riding into a haze of unreality. He felt a vague surprise when the mare under him turned off the trail into a small stream, following the other horse, and then came up the bank further on to stop in the trees. He sat there stupidly as the woman dismounted.

"Get down," she said. "We'll camp here for the day."

He wakened slightly as she reached up to untie her pack, and managed to slide down without falling. He had to catch the stirrup leather and lean against the saddle until his head stopped spinning. Luckily the mare was tired, too, and she endured that until he felt well enough to push away from her.

"Take care of the horses," the woman ordered him, holding out the reins of hers, and belatedly he reached and took them. It was something his body could do automatically, without any need for thought. He couldn't move his left arm at all and he was limping heavily and felt dull and dizzy again, but he had no objections. The kria always cared for the horses before themselves.

His hands fumbled and his fingers felt weak, but still he was able to slip the bits and loosen the girths to let the animals drink. He untied his own pack and dropped it in the bracken. Then he drank and rested with his head down, waiting for the horses to finish, tethered them in the shade where he could slide the saddles off without having to lift or carry them anywhere. He found feed in the saddlebags, and with the absence of much forage nearby, he measured out some for each of them. There seemed to be no particular tools for it, so he rubbed the animals down briefly with leaves and fern before he left them alone. Then he sat down where he was and dropped his head on his knees.

The woman had gathered a pile of sticks and started a small fire, sat feeding the dry wood into it gradually.

"What's wrong with your arm?" she asked.

He moved his head slightly. "It hurts," he said.

"I guessed that," she said. "I want to know why. Is it strained? Or a wound?"

"A wound," he said.

She threw a bigger log on the flames and rose, wiping her hands on her skirt.

"Let me see it," she said.

He eased the jacket off, but the shirt was stuck to the wound.

"I can't," he said.

She stood over him and tugged at the fabric, investigating the problem as if she didn't believe what he'd said. He winced at the dart of pain that ran through his shoulder.

"Stay here," she said then, letting go. "There's blood on it."

He had expected that. He laid his head down again without really caring and drifted away as she busied herself with the fire. He came awake sometime later as a hot compress fell against his shoulder, on the shirt and all.

"Be still," she said, at his start. "I'm going to soak it off."

It took some time and some pain, but the shirt did come off, leaving the scent of wet, hot wool drifting in his nostrils. He felt the warm blood flow down his back when she tugged it loose. When she pushed the compress against the wound to stop that, he jerked and had to bite his lip to stifle a cry. It hurt for her to touch the skin anywhere near it and the whole shoulder throbbed, raw and inflamed. Once started, the pain knifed down his arm and back, and up into his skull with an agonizing pulse.

"It looks infected," she said, uncertainly. "Is this an arrow wound?"

It was. The arrow had been nearly spent and had struck his shoulder without enough force to punch through, but it had cut into the flesh and bone painfully. The point hadn't been fine in the first place and his captors had wrenched it out without much care. He knew it must be an ugly wound, though it couldn't be very deep.

She spread a blanket on the ground for him. "The point must have been filthy," she said. "Lie down."

He did, glad enough to get his head on the solid earth. He wanted to sleep, but exhausted as he was, he knew he wouldn't ever achieve it—everything hurt too much. He could only drift back into the confused half-consciousness that had afflicted him the night before, only pulsing now with white-hot pain.

She was back beside him, laid the warm compress on his bare skin. It burned like fire this time, and he started and gasped and reached for it, but she caught his fingers.

"Leave it alone," she said. "That's just salt in the water. It'll hurt less after a while, and it will draw the infection out."

He lay there and concentrated on breathing. After a while the burning eased off and she let go of his hand, went back to the fire. The smell of cooking rose, and when she came back again she had brought a wooden bowl for him.

"Sit up," she said, and when he had struggled up, she threw another blanket around his shoulders and handed him the food. It was stew and fried bread, and should have been more to his taste than the milk and cheese had been last night, but he couldn't eat. He tried some of the stew and couldn't chew it, and the smell of the bread made him ill. He let the bowl down beside him and eased his aching head down on his knee, found the woman was watching him.

"Don't you want it?" she asked.

"No," he whispered.

She came and took it out of his hand.

"Are you going to faint?" she asked, seeming concerned, and he thought then he must look as ill as he felt. "Lie back down," she said, and when he did, she laid her hand against his face. It was a direct, no-nonsense move that he hadn't any chance to evade.

"You're hot," she said, taking her hand away. But she was wrong; he was shivering with cold. "Can you drink willow tea?"

"Yes," he said, and was hardly even aware that she went away. She seemed to be back immediately with another hot compress for his shoulder, and with the bitter tea, which he sat up to drink.

She watched him, looking tired and angry.

"Something should have been done about this yesterday," she said.

He didn't think that was his fault. He hadn't exactly been in a position to do anything about it himself.

"Lie down again," she said then. "At least there's water. Maybe we can stay here a day or two."

He thought she paced in front of the fire, and after a while she came to change the compress again.

"I have some salve that might take the sting out of the burns," she said at some time or the other. When he murmured something of assent, she brought it, rubbed it on with distressing familiarity. It did seem to help, and numbed the hurt a little. "Any more of them?" she asked.

"Yes," he said. It was the ones on the insides of his thighs that had made riding such an agony, but she didn't offer to undress him to get at those.

"I'll leave it here for later," she said. "Maybe I have something for the cuts, too." She went off searching for that.

She continued to pace and to sit next to him periodically, and he became aware she looked more exhausted and irritable as the sun climbed higher through the trees, and then later began to fall toward dusk. She seemed to contain an urge to put her hands on him, perhaps to check for the fever, but by that time he hardly cared what she did. He only wished she would go away—to sleep herself, maybe—and leave him alone with his misery, so he didn't have to be aware all the time that she was there.

"I hope to hell you're worth this delay," she said once, apparently to herself. "This could damn well mean trouble."

He couldn't remember what delay she meant. Then the thought intruded that he wasn't worth anything and wouldn't ever be again. He meant to say that, but he couldn't get the words out and drifted off instead into confused, feverish dreams. He felt bewildered and helpless, and would rather have crept away to die alone in the brush. But later he did feel clearer, as perhaps the fever broke, and he fell away into a real sleep, and didn't know any more whether she was there or not.

It was night when he woke, and cooking smells drifted on the wood smoke again. After a while Cybelle's step crunched on the fern near his head, spreading their sweet spice into the air.

"Are you awake?" she asked, and knelt beside him. Her voice sounded kinder now, and he thought she must have slept, herself.

She had brought him a bowl of broth to drink this time. "I made more stew," she said, "if you feel like eating."

He drank the broth and ate some of the stew with bread, and then he struggled up and went into the woods, taking the salve to put on his legs. It seemed to have done what she promised for his back and sides. The burns there still hurt, but not like they had. His shoulder felt better, too, only an ordinary ache now, and not the fiery inflammation that had made him so ill. But he was still weak, and cold even with the blanket around him. He came back and let that fall, found the wool shirt and slid it on carefully over his shoulders and then wrapped in the blanket again. He wouldn't try the jacket for a while.

The stew would simmer on the fire overnight for them to eat tomorrow, but the pan for the bread should be cleaned. He hobbled up to the fire and reached for it, meaning to carry it to the stream and scrub it with sand, but the woman put her hand on it instead.

"No," she said. "I'll do it. Sit down."

It surprised him, but he didn't say anything, only wrapped the blanket tighter around his shoulders and ducked his head to sit by the fire, glad of its warmth. The woman came back from washing the pan and put it away in her gear, all still packed, as if she thought they might have to leave in a hurry. It was the same caution he might have used, but still he noticed it. Humans weren't usually so careful.

"I take it you're feeling better," she said, sitting down uncomfortably close to him.

He flicked his fingers in a signal for "yes," and then realized it was a kria gesture that she wouldn't recognize. So he said the word in her language, wondering if it would be an affront to edge away from her.

"If you're at all grateful for the effort I've expended to help you," she said, "then please try to help me in return."

He glanced at her sideways and saw that her eyes were very dark in the firelight. He didn't ask how he could help her, fearing what it would be, but she didn't wait for him to ask. She leaned over and began to draw lines with a stick in the soft dirt where she had cleared the ground cover to build a fire.

"I don't know this country," she said, "beyond where we are now. Tell me what you know about it."

She pointed to her drawing. "Here's the river that's to the north of us," she said. "Start there."

He was immediately lost.

He had an excellent command of the humans' language as far as understanding went, much better than most of his people. He had recently made a study of humans, and there were few things they said that he didn't know of. From more experience than usual in dealing with them as enemies, he could follow the alien thought patterns, and often even infer concepts. The sounds of the language flowed over his tongue relatively well. But still, he had never really spoken with them, never had to generate information, or to organize it into real, coherent speech.

She grew quickly impatient.

"Woman, please..." he said, as she snapped at him.

"My name is Cybelle."

"Lhassa," he said then. The clan leaders of his own people were female, and the term of respect came easily to his tongue, safer perhaps than groping in the human language for something appropriate. He could not address her by name, witch or ayeen as she might be. It was a terrifying idea. "Please, I don't know the words," he explained, admitting his deficiency.

She studied him then, as if this difficulty hadn't occurred to her.

"I thought..." she began. "Well, you understand me well enough," she said, and then seemed to reconsider, suddenly doubtful. "Or do you?"

"Yes," he said, "without too many problems. But making the words, lhassa..."

She shifted her eyes suddenly, stared at the fire.

"I'm being unreasonable," she said, and sighed. She tossed the stick she had been drawing with into the flames. The point had broken off as she shoved it against the ground. "I didn't think." But then she turned back to him. "You speak the language very well," she said, facing him squarely, and then she turned again and went back to work on the drawing with a different stick. She hadn't given up, of course. She only seemed more determined. Still it occurred to him that he might have heard an apology, unlikely as it was. The idea surprised him.

"What's beside the river in the forest here?" she asked. "Are there villages?"

This was easier, the vacuum filled by specific questions, and he understood the drawing after a moment of studying the perspectives, told her of what human villages he knew locally, and how far the warriors from them ranged.

"What's behind us, over here?" she asked, gesturing to the west.

"Mountains," he said.

"What elevation?"

He searched for the answer. "High enough for snow most of the year." It seemed to satisfy her well enough. He was doing better now, following the way her mind worked, at least to a certain extent. "There are people that live there, too, and they keep sheep and trade with the villages of the valley."

"How many days ride to get there?"

"About five full days," he said.

"What's beyond the mountains?" she asked.

"Wastelands, my people say. I have never been there. The rains come from the river and the sea further east— here." He reached out and added the curved edge of it to the drawing with one finger. "The rains seldom go past the mountains."

She looked at him with eyes that seemed piercing.

"How easy is it to get across the mountains this time of the year by horse?"

"There is a pass, lhassa, which will be open now with the spring, so that riders might go through. Other than that I don't know. There are the mountain villages, and baywolves, and perhaps late storms that would all be dangers."

"What's downriver in the direction we're going?"

"More forest," he said, and found his thoughts were completely even now. "Different villages. Eventually the sea."

"You know the villages?"

"Some, lhassa."

"And where is your village, Ta Nyahl?"

It stopped the words in his throat, and he stared at her in terror that she would insist to know that, dropped his face against his knees.

"And we were doing so well," she commented.

He stayed silent.

"Never mind," she said. "Forget it. Probably I can get by without knowing. After all, I've been here a while, and didn't even realize you existed. Nobody's said a word...An invisible people, and a mystery for sure. What we'll do about it..."

When he risked a glance up, she only seemed to be thinking, staring into the firelight, but her lips were tight.

They stayed camped where they were. The woman Cybelle asked him to stand first watch, making him ashamed that he'd been so weak and unable to do it as she slept during the day. She must have been exhausted, and perhaps had risked their safety in order to rest. Tonight she made her bed so near the horses that she risked injury, he thought, and he wondered what it was that she distrusted, whether it was him, or whether she thought he would fall asleep and let others come down on her. Whatever, the movement of the horses would wake her if anything crept too close. He shifted from time to time, trying to get comfortable, but not too much so. His shoulder began to ache with cold as the fire died lower. The night was quiet. The spring calls of the don'will assured him the woods were undisturbed. Now and then a rustle passed close by, a blue fox and later matins investigating the scent. A spatter of rain passed, and then as the moons began to fall, Cybelle woke and kept watch while he rested.

He slept almost too heavily, and woke in daylight feeling miserably stiff and sore, but still better and without the fever. A fog lay on the ground, risen up from the reeds. The cloud on the earth was unusual for this time of year, and the air was colder after the rain. He pushed up with an effort, tried to flex some of the soreness out of his muscles, and then limped off carefully to check and feed the horses. There wasn't much grain left in the saddlebags. They would have to move eventually to find pasture, if nothing else. The delay here might sharply reduce some of their supplies, especially if there had been only provisions for one. He wondered if that was what the woman had meant by her comment as he'd lain ill—something about a delay—or if there had been something else.

Chapter 4

After Ta Nyahl had seen to the horses, he went down to the water to wash, and when he came back, Cybelle had the fire rekindled and water added to freshen the stew. It appeared she meant to cook bread for breakfast. She glanced up as he appeared, with the dark, unreadable glance he was getting used to, as if she didn't mean for him to see through it to what she really thought. Likely it was a discomfort with him, he thought, or with what he was. That would certainly be natural in a human. He wondered at her tolerance.

"Let me see your shoulder," she said, and he unlaced the shirt, eased it partially off to show the wound to her. "It looks better," she commented. Then she fastened the compress pad, now dried and heated by the fire, inside his shirt to keep the wool from abrading the wound. "I don't have anything to use for bandages," she said. "But maybe that will protect it some." And it felt better, the hot pad making it more comfortable, at least for a while, until the cold started slipping in again.

This morning Ta Nyahl had awakened sharply concerned about the position he would have to live in now. A sense of low-grade nightmare continued, almost surreal. He knew his life would never be the same again, never honorable enough that he could have the comfort of familiar things, the customs of his childhood. That was a given now, but as his head cleared, he began to wonder what he could expect from the woman.

His own people didn't keep slaves, even had problems understanding the concept of personal ownership—they tended to share possessions—and he'd had to learn by hard experience what the humans meant by it. Of course humans did keep slaves, captives of other clans, and sometimes children or women without protection who were taken by force or to satisfy debts. He knew they treated all their slaves poorly, beat and starved or sometimes disfigured them for no reason. It was a degraded status, and a slave couldn't expect any kindness, or even reasonable treatment. If he had been set to slavery in the village they had just left, he wouldn't have survived for very long. But to his surprise, this woman had gone to a considerable effort to allow him to rest and had even cared for his wounds when she apparently wanted instead to travel—and she hadn't abandoned him. It was a situation that he didn't understand, and now he was worrying about witchcraft again. There might be demands beyond anything he was familiar with, and dangers to his soul. At that thought, he whispered a prayer to the spirits of his ancestors to watch over him.

Cybelle seemed an ordinary woman to look at, only somewhat different in manner from other human women that he knew of—perhaps less cruel. She must be a witch to travel as she did, alone in the forest—that was often dangerous even for a man. And if she were definitely a witch, there must be hidden dangers in dealing with her.

With the little increase in his strength came bitterness, but also a need to know where they were going and what would be required of him. So he knelt before her respectfully, keeping his eyes on the ground, and prepared to ask.

"Lhassa?"

She looked at him pointedly, and he felt his face grow hot. His resolve almost failed, but he'd known it would be difficult to ask so directly, as humans expected.

"Lhassa," he said again. "How do you wish for me to serve you?"

Her eyes were hard as stone.

"Just obey me," she said irritably. "And don't cause me any problems. Other than that, you don't need to worry about it." She looked angry then, as if she thought he wouldn't be able to do those simple things. She jabbed sternly at the bread cakes with a sharpened stick.

He blinked, embarrassed, and thought it must have been a forward question, one that showed doubt of her motives perhaps, or her ability to direct their progress. Maybe she thought he meant to renege on his oath—maybe that he meant to harm her, or steal her supplies and ride away. In light of his oath, that was painful, but still understandable, and in dealing with her, he expected to be affronted. Surely he would make mistakes and suffer for them. He had been braced for a sharp reply, after all. He accepted the rebuke and only took a slightly deeper breath before trying again.

"Lhassa, please. It may not be easy for you to travel through human country with me along."

He said that because of his memory of her expression when she'd first seen his face. Something about it worried him, as if she'd never seen the like before, and was completely unfamiliar with his people. If that were so, maybe she had come from over the mountains herself, or from somewhere across the river to the north, where rumor of the kria hadn't gone. Maybe she wouldn't know how relations were between the kria and humans. It felt awkward even to discuss that, humiliating in the way it brought up bloody memories, and all the ways that humans had hurt his people.

She looked at him straight this time, appraisingly, and he waited, bearing the weight of her eyes.

"You're likely to get that same reception everywhere?" she asked. "Well. I'm not surprised, considering," she went on. And then she sighed, suddenly pensive. "Ta Nyahl, what if I just send you back to your own people?"

His eyes widened in horror, flickered up in spite of his resolve not to look at her directly. He caught his breath. "Lhassa..." he protested, suddenly galvanized with fear, and then stopped.

"Why not?" she asked sharply. She was holding the stick almost defensively now, as if to fend him away with it.

"I can't go back," he said simply.

"Why can't you?" she demanded.

He stumbled then, inundated with reasons and at once unable to put any of them into human words. He only made a faint sound of denial instead, terrified at the abyss that lay in that direction, at the idea of being adrift without purpose and without kin. He covered his face with his hands.

"Are you damned by swearing an oath to me?" she guessed.

It was very perceptive, and that was part of the problem. It was easier to admit it once he thought she might understand. He dropped his hands, flicked his fingers weakly, then remembered to say the words.

"In a way, lhassa," he said. "No kria has ever served a human, and certainly it is an offense against all my ancestors, but I swore I would do it and so I will. I can't go back to my people. I have to stay with you and fulfill my promise, and when you're done with me then I will die."

She looked alarmed. "What the hell for?" she asked.

His face was hot again. But he was being truthful. It was the only eventual solution to this problem that he could see. He tried to put the reasons into words.

"I'm not worth anything alone, lhassa. There isn't a place for me outside the clans. I can't live that way."

She seemed to think about that, and then she threw the stick down.

"Dammit," she said. She rubbed her palms over her face, dug the heels of her hands into her eyes. "What have I gotten myself into now?" she asked.

But then she swung around to face him, so suddenly that he flinched.

"All right," she said, sounding ordinary again, as if she had this in perspective now, and had placed it secondary to her purpose. "Come with me, then. I need someone to help me travel. We're going to the mountains. We'll have to beware of the villages, but I'd just as soon do that anyway. I'll decide what to do about you later. Just don't talk to me about a death wish, do you hear? I have problems enough of my own, and I don't want to hear about it," she said.

"But how do you wish for me to serve you?" he persisted, and expected her to snap at him again.

She sighed instead, only infinitely weary.

"Ride with me," she said then, simply. "Take care of the horses and the chores, if you will. Watch my back so I can sleep at night."

He thought again of how she had made her bed at the horses' feet.

"Lhassa," he said, staring down respectfully, not daring to look at her face, and suggested, "It might be more helpful if I had weapons."

Quietly he gripped his hands in the folds of the leather skirt, waiting for her to answer. This was important to him.

"No," she said emphatically. And that was the end of that. It had been too much to expect anyway, and it defined his status clearly enough. The bread was burning by then, and she took it off the fire, handed him a bowl of stew.

"Here," she said. "Eat. If you feel up to traveling, we'll leave at dusk."

"Yes, lhassa," he said, and did as he was told.

He sat against a tree and drowsed in the sun while she cleaned the cooking pots, resting while he could, but he was aware that Cybelle paced, frowning and restless, and he thought now that she watched him sometimes, appraisingly still. Beginning to grope for life again, he felt naked without weapons, without at least the bone-handled knife he had carried since childhood, which the humans had taken from him. But there seemed to be little trust in this woman, regardless that he'd sworn his life to her. It was a symptom of the humans' relations with one another, he decided, that they couldn't trust anyone.

He slid down and fell asleep finally. He slept soundly for a while and woke stiff again, but there was nothing to do about that until his bruises had healed. It was still a long time until evening, so he took a walk along the stream bank, listening to the sounds of the forest and looking for round stones to put in his pockets. There were dried reeds a little way along the stream bank, and he tore some out of the shallows and stripped the fibers to braid into twine. He meant to tie back his hair. The lhassa might have something better he could use for it, perhaps a leather thong—but he wouldn't ask for anything now. Her distrust had set up a barrier between them that was for the moment insurmountable. Perhaps that was because of what he was, after all—a slave who would likely resent that status, and also different from her, so that she couldn't feel confident in predicting what he would do.

He found a certain contentment in sitting in the cloudy light of late morning working with his hands—a few small, mindless moments that he could snatch from the situation. He could pretend for a while that he sat in camp with one of his own people, but cold reality kept intruding, the scent of the human woman not far away. And the chill was growing literal as well as figurative. As he sat there, he felt the cold drift of a breeze that swirled down the streambed, wind rising after the preliminary rain, and he smelled snow on it. The reading was subliminal, but sure. The weather would turn worse in the night—perhaps they ought to seek shelter instead of trying to travel. Then the gust carried more than air alone. His fingers froze on the twine.

It had been an intelligent move for Cybelle to turn off the track at the stream crossing. It confused their trail for anyone who might follow. It wouldn't stop a determined tracker if one were following them, but it would slow one down, who would then have to cast up and down the stream for the place where they had left the water. Still, it had only been a marginal caution. She hadn't come far enough down or made any real effort to hide the camp. Cybelle likely had only intended to stay for a short time, and now suddenly her impatience made sense to him. A chill ran down his spine as he felt the shape of things she hadn't told him. There were men following her, and the two of them had lingered here too long.

He eased up to his feet, stuffed the fibers into a pocket of the jacket. As quietly as he could move in the heavy leather that clothed him, he retraced his steps up the creek and slid over to where she sat by the fire. Apparently she was far distant in some thoughts of her own. She turned absently as he knelt beside her.

"Lhassa," he whispered. "There are men following behind us on the trail. They're at the crossing." And then he watched her, to find how she would react.

She started visibly. A shock went over her face, but then her eyes narrowed.

"How do you know?" she asked.

"The wind," he whispered, insistent now that he knew her fear.

She looked at him in disbelief.

"Please, I just know," he said, and then recklessly, he put out a hand, stopped short of touching her. "Lhassa..."

He hadn't any time to explain. Maybe the rain had covered the horses' prints, and maybe not. If it was obvious which way they had turned, then human enemies could find them in minutes. He was sure now they wouldn't be her friends. He turned, galvanized, and rapidly began to scoop dirt onto the fire to kill the smoke.

"Will you take the chance I don't know?" he asked.

She moved suddenly. Apparently she wouldn't.

"Saddle the horses," she said, reaching to roll up her pack.

"No," he protested. He struggled after her, caught her fingers on the ties, forgetting in his desperation that he'd meant not to touch her. "Better only to be still." When she stared at him, he blundered on. "There's not time enough to go, lhassa. If we make a noise, they will find us. And if we're still, they may go by. Please, only take the horses and hide in the trees."

She considered it.

"All right," she said, but she tied up the pack anyway, and carried it across the clearing and dropped it near the horses. Then she knelt by the saddles. He thought she took something out of her saddlebag before she grasped the horses' leads and led them behind a screen of rocks and brush.

She was well enough hidden there. He thought she'd be better able to control the horses if someone came along the stream searching for them if he kept his distance. The animals were still afraid of him, so he took care to fade into the trees downwind before he circled back to the water and slid down the bank. That way his scent wouldn't make them restless and give away their position. He sank into in a growth of reeds that clattered softly in the wind and waited, hoping the woman could be patient, too. It was the way of his people to let danger go by without waste of life or effort, if they could help it. The kria wouldn't stand and fight unless forced to it.

In a moment he caught the sounds of mounted men drifting along the stream, a faint jingle of harness, a murmur of voices carrying down the wind. They stopped at the crossing, and he held his breath for fear the horses would scent them, but they came no closer. He stayed crouching by the water's edge, his eyes closed in concentration, gathering what information he could from sound and scent over the distance.

It was a large party, eight men, and he thought they wouldn't be honest hunters riding after a woman this way. There weren't quite enough of them for a raiding party, but perhaps they had lost some of their number in a fight. Apparently they had only stopped to water their horses, because soon they made sounds of mounting up and fading away down the track. Ta Nyahl let out his breath at that.

The men had been careless and unobservant, from the way they had moved—but that wasn't unusual for humans. And if there had been prints of their own horses left from the rain, they were covered now—the large, awkward party would have trampled over them. Ta Nyahl stayed where he was until the sounds faded beyond any doubt, then he straightened finally from concealment and began the climb back up the rocky bank.

One of the horses snorted as he neared the trees.

"Lhassa?" he called softly. "They are gone."

She appeared from behind the brush fiercely, with eyes that were like dark storm clouds.

"Saddle the horses," she said. "We're leaving now."

The thing she had taken from the saddlebag was still in her hand. She had kept it hidden in the folds of her skirt, but now as she turned away she slid it into a pocket under her jacket, and he caught sight of it. It hadn't been a covert move that she made. She hadn't expected him to recognize it, but he did. For an instant he stared as it was exposed. He blinked, knowing not the thing itself, nor even the specific workmanship, but knowing it was alien in this place. Then he bent and caught up one of the saddles.

She hesitated, half-turned. She had glimpsed his hesitation, but perhaps he had hidden his startlement well enough. She only gave him a sharp glance and hurried to gather up her pack. Then she reached for the horses' heads. The mare had already laid back her ears and swung her head to bite Ta Nyahl, and now she rolled her eyes evilly, trying to jerk from under the saddle as he lifted it.

The tack was less of a fight with Cybelle's help in holding the mare, and he was ready for the animal's quick sidestep this time as he tried to mount. He compensated, made it to the saddle with only a slight catch of breath as his knees met the leather. He tightened the reins to control any further protests, and then looked at Cybelle for instructions.

"We need to go west," said Cybelle. "Lead off however you want."

He considered that, momentarily confused. He decided she was deferring to his knowledge of the country, leaving the decision of how to travel up to him. Ahead now on the trail they had left were enemies—to him definitely, and also, apparently, to Cybelle. If they were tracking her, they'd likely realize they had lost the trail and come back to cast for it. If heading that way had ever had been a good idea, it wasn't any more—and he had doubted it before. He glanced around at the trees, the stream. A gust of wind buffeted him, dragged his hair before his eyes. With a harsh cry, a kelbird skimmed through the clearing, unbalanced by the sudden turbulence. It was concrete evidence of weather moving in.

To anyone searching, their camp here by the water was easily visible, with little way to hide it. Worse, it would be visible even after a hard rain. The bracken was trampled and torn and the shrubs stripped by the horses for forage. The ashes of the fire were fresh, and cooking grease was burnt into the soil. He glanced up stream, thought about going that way a distance before they struck out to the west, but decided it wouldn't do much to hide their direction. Northward, the stream narrowed quickly. So he turned the mare toward the south and downstream instead, using the water as the best cover available.

"This way," he said.

The water would grow deep later on as another stream joined it, but they could camp twice more on the bank before they had to turn west for the mountains. Plus, they would have the water along the way. It was a better choice than turning directly west. It was only later that it occurred to him that Cybelle probably wanted him ahead of her so she could watch him.

Riding the horse was automatic, and his mind considered what he was doing. He searched, and found his concepts of reality were crumbling. Like aftershocks to the initial disaster of his capture and his loss of Da Hanath and Da Kathan, the world kept rearranging in ways he couldn't predict. He'd thought he didn't care any more about what happened to him. He'd expected to die inside somehow, with his oath, had thought that afterward nothing would ever affect him again.

Now he found himself alive and reasonably well, and struggling to make sense of things, as if it really mattered one way or the other. Perhaps it was a survival instinct that made him search for meanings and forced him to be aware of implications. However disoriented he was, logic served him yet, and now a curious tension had developed between him and this woman. It provoked him that she was keeping him ignorant of whatever dangers were after her. It endangered him, too, and aggravated his bitterness. But there was more to it that just that. She wasn't what she seemed. And he thought now he knew why her people called her a witch.

His mare was sure-footed, regardless of her shortfalls in temperament, but she slipped suddenly on the mossy creek stones, jolted him painfully. The travel was uncomfortable. Even though the streambed was cut deeply into the soil and rock, still he had to roll and duck more often than was comfortable to avoid low-slung limbs and grasping thickets. His shoulder began to ache persistently, and his burns began to sting. The wind lashed at them. By mid-afternoon rain began to blow in cold sheets along the water.

Ta Nyahl thought there would be ice soon along the rocks, forming like knives to cut at the horses' fetlocks. He started to shiver, and to worry seriously about the weather. He hoped Cybelle would be willing to stop at dusk to camp again.

It turned out that she was. The sky dimmed well before night and sleet began to sting their faces. Temperature dropped like a stone. Perhaps Cybelle could feel the change in pressure from the storm, feel the horses' fear as they strained against the wind. Her own gelding seemed less sure than the mare. He had stumbled twice and come near to throwing her into the icy water. They could hardly afford that kind of disaster now.

Chapter 5

The storm only got worse. Ta Nyahl wasn't pleased at the sudden death of light, and the sharpness of the gale that tossed the trees above their heads. He could smell death on the wind now. It was a dangerous storm, and it would be fatal to be caught by darkness without shelter. He began to look desperately for a place to leave the stream, found a low, muddy spot in the rocks. From the prints it was a watering place for deer. He forced his mare up the bank into the teeth of the gale. She snorted and balked as she felt the lash of it. The bay gelding followed behind with its rider, only a shadow now in the sleet, seen from the corner of his eye. The watering place would mark another trail that he expected to run roughly east and west. He turned sharply west and led on until they were away from the soft ground. Then he urged the mare into a trot, seeking for rocks, brush—any sheltered spot to ride out the storm. Rain slanted sideways, and wind struck them in earnest, tearing limbs from the trees. His wet hair whipped at his face, and he twisted the cold strands with one hand, tried to tuck them into the jacket. That didn't last, and soon the whips of it were in his eyes again.

Thankfully, the horses came up against a rocky ridge, and Ta Nyahl began to look for a space in the rocks. They had to find protection from the blizzard soon. Debris was flying from the broken trees, along with icy clots of snow. He chose a likely spot as well as he could through the knife-edged curtain of sleet and intervening brush, a crevice in the stone leading upward. Then he turned in the saddle, ready to take the risk of asking. He was tiring rapidly now, and he desperately needed to rest. He knew the horses did, too.

"Lhassa," he shouted above the wind, protecting his eyes with one hand, "the storm will last many hours, and we need what shelter we can find. Will you stop here?" He was asking her permission as if she were a clan leader of his own people, thinking it was wise, and a way to avoid argument.

"Stop," she acquiesced, shouting over the wind. "It's about time." He thought perhaps her teeth were chattering from the cold. Her voice sounded uneven.

He dismounted painfully, stiffened by the cold and numb with misery. The mare sidestepped and nearly knocked him over, swinging her hindquarters suddenly, turning tail to the buffet of wind. The gelding was limping, he saw, as he gathered the reins of both and hauled at them, leading the horses through the trees and toward the shelter of a slanted overhang he had dimly glimpsed, almost read in the lay of the rocks. Unexpectedly he crossed a trail, turned onto it. The mare slipped in the mud, jerked him backward. He swung around to look, saw that Cybelle was still with him, clinging to the bay's stirrup.

She wiped the icy rain from her face.

"Where to?" she shouted.

He quickly scanned the cliffs, picked out a way.

"There," he cried, pointing.

It appeared only a darker shadow in the dusk, but as they approached, he could see it was better than he could have dared hope. It was a cleft, if not a deeper cave, and the entrance was tall enough even for the horses.

Cybelle made some exclamation and started forward, but he called her back.

"Wait! Let me check first," he shouted.

He left her with the horses and ducked into the space, found it went several spans back before closing to nothing. The smell of a las bear lingered, heavy and close, and there were broken bones and debris, but they were old. He went back to the opening, reached to take the reins from Cybelle.

"It's clear," he said. "Come in."

There was dry tinder and kindling in one of the packs, but they would need logs to wait out a blizzard of any length. He was shivering and exhausted and aching with cold, but he didn't want to freeze without enough fuel for a fire. He wrapped his arms around his belly under the jacket, trying to warm his icy hands against his ribs. He was shivering violently.

"I will bring wood, lhassa," he said, hearing his voice echo off the rock and disappear in the hiss of sleet across the entrance. There seemed to be a catch in it, the shadings of exhaustion. He closed his eyes. "...if you will give me your axe..."

She had apparently classified that implement with other weapons heretofore, and kept it away from him. Now she jerked her pack off the horse and dropped it awkwardly. She tugged open the bindings and dragged the short-handled hatchet out from its leather case, handed it to him without comment.

He plunged out into the weather, dragging the unwilling mare behind him. The flying sleet was turning to a wet snow. Down the slope he found a fallen tree, mid-sized. He hacked at the larger branches, heaved the logs up and roped them to the saddle. He could hardly carry enough wood under these conditions to last a day. If the storm continued, he would have to come back later when the drifts formed like deep waves between the trees and trapped them within the cave. It would be easier to cut the wood then, when the wind had died down.

The gale tore at him now, whipping the dark curtain of hair before his eyes. He twisted and tucked it again, but it wouldn't stay. He dragged at the mare, leading her up the hill through evergreens already weighted with snow and heavy with ice.

He slipped on mud below the cave entrance and fell. Pain lanced through his shoulder as he caught himself on the weak arm, and he lost the reins. The mare must be as frozen and weary as he was. She only tossed her head in startlement as he slid. She waited for him to get up, catch the reins and labor on. Nearly blind, he found himself suddenly at the lip of the cave, and he would have stood there in disbelief, but the mare crowded him from behind and shoved him in. He stamped the snow and mud from his boots at the cave entrance, reached to unlash the wood and drop it by a fire already laid. Cybelle moved from where she had stood back to watch him come in. It was only when she had the axe back in her hands that she finally knelt and lit the tinder with her flint and steel.

"I didn't know how long you'd be," she said, as if in explanation. But he'd understood her caution in that regard already. Dry kindling was a luxury she couldn't afford to waste.

The mare shook herself suddenly, spattering mud and icy water over them. The tiny fire hissed and spat, and Cybelle cursed.

"For God's sake, do something about her, will you?"

Cybelle had the bay already settled, the ice rubbed from his coat with the saddle blanket. Ta Nyahl unsaddled the mare with the last of his strength, found he was staggering as he dropped the tack into a pile near Cybelle's. He leaned against the wall for a moment, then rubbed the mare down roughly and gave both the horses feed. Then he slid down the cold wall and rolled onto his belly, laid his head down on the rock in limp exhaustion.

After a moment he realized Cybelle must have said something to him, and that he hadn't answered. She left the fire to stand over him.

"Are you all right?" she asked.

"What?" he managed, faintly.

"Don't go to sleep like that," she said. "Get out of the wet clothes."

"Yes," he agreed. But he didn't move. He was too numb even to shiver. His hair lay over his face in wet strands and the leather he wore was frigid, wet through as it was. Even the wool beneath was icy.

Cybelle continued to stand there.

"Are you going to get up?" She sounded worried.

He lay, still numb, and after a moment she nudged him sharply with the cold toe of her boot.

"Ta Nyahl."

He stirred, realizing numbly that she wouldn't let him rest. He shoved painfully to a sitting position, let his head fall on his knees. It seemed to satisfy her. She stepped away from him, transferred a log to the growing fire that sizzled and popped as the wet boiled away. She had laid the kindling well, far enough from the opening that rain wouldn't touch it. But apparently there was enough ventilation from the crevice in back of them that the grotto wouldn't fill with smoke, either, at least not enough to choke them. It rose and filmed the ceiling in swirling patterns, but the air stayed clear beneath.

The space was small for them and the animals, too, and quickly it had filled with the stable scent of wet horses, the comfortable sounds of crunching grain. It would be dangerous if the animals bolted or panicked in the tight confines, but exhausted as they were tonight, that was hardly likely. And left outside, they might freeze in the storm—certainly a disaster to be avoided. Out there, darkness was falling faster than the snow. Wind howled around the formations above them, swayed the trees violently within view of the entrance. Cold swirled through the cave opening now and again, guttering the flames that licked about the wet wood like golden ghosts.

There wasn't any real privacy in such shallow quarters, but Cybelle went behind the horses and he heard her clothing open and drop, then a rummaging in the saddlebags as she searched for something warm to wear. She emerged wrapped in wool, a blanket fastened at the shoulder with the pin from her cloak. She spread her leather to dry as well as she could and came to stand over the fire again, scrubbing at her hair to dry it. Loose now and darkened with the wet, it hung down in surprisingly fine, damp curls.

"You do the same," she said, pointedly. "I don't want you freezing to death."

Having rested the few minutes, he was about equal to the task now, and dragged himself up to repeat her performance, except that he hadn't any pin to fasten the blanket around him. He was shivering by then—maybe an improvement. Filled with cold and misery, he lay down again as Cybelle clattered the cooking utensils. Soon she was frying bread and onions.

"Are you awake?" she asked.

He came back from a sodden half-consciousness to find her standing over him, holding a bowl. It was full night and fire shadows danced on the walls, outlined the dark shapes of the horses. A certain warmth had come to the cave, and it seemed almost comfortable as he sat by the fire to eat. Snow and sleet pelted through the opening from time to time on a swirl of wind, enough to impress Ta Nyahl with the luxuries of their shelter, rude and shallow as it was. With warm food in his belly, he felt quite a bit better. He estimated that this storm was worse than some, and thought of what it would have been like to die in it.

Perhaps Cybelle was thinking something of the same. From time to time her eyes strayed away from the fire to fix on the violent darkness that filled the world outside.

"I think you've earned your keep," she said finally, breaking the silence.

He looked up to find her eyes on him, dark and challenging. He couldn't find anything to say in reply.

"If I were out there alone, I'd be dead," she went on, sopping gravy from her bowl with a chunk of bread. "I wouldn't have recognized the dangers in time. And I'd never have found this place to shelter in."

He stared at the flames, forgetting to eat.

"Thank you," she said.

He was ashamed to think her thanks were unwarranted. "It was only panic, lhassa. I meant to save my own life."

"Still..." she said, and let the thought trail away. She started and glanced at the opening again at an ominous crack and crash from the trees below. Wind screaming through the rocks above them had broken one of the trees. He thought she shuddered, and her chest heaved with a sudden breath. "Are these storms common here?"

"They come sometimes," he said, "in from the sea."

She pressed her lips together in response. "Another delay."

"Will that be a problem, lhassa?" he asked.

"It depends," she hedged, and moved restlessly at some hidden thoughts. "How long will this last?"

"Only a day or two," he said. "The ground is too warm now for the snow to stay on it for very long."

"Two days?" She shifted her head to watch the spatter of wet snow beyond the fire.

"Maybe only one," he said. "It came up very fast, and maybe it will finish tonight or early tomorrow."

Silence fell between them, and he studied the bowl in his hands.

"Will the men follow us, lhassa?"

She frowned, laid down her bowl and stretched her hands to the fire. Still, she accepted the question with better grace than he'd expected.

"I hope to hell they all die in this storm," she said. But she didn't give him any details about why she hoped so.

She pushed up suddenly, stacked her bowl with the frying pan, and went to wash her hands in the snow.

"Since you've rested," she said wearily, "will you clean up and take first watch?"

"Yes," he said, still staring at his bowl.

Grateful though she might be, she still chose a place near the horses for her bed.

Sitting cross-legged by the fire, he listened as her quiet breathing joined that of the horses. He thought of the weariness he had seen in her, and a glimpse of something else that she kept hidden in the back of her eyes. He thought he knew what it was—the slowness of their progress and the declining level of rations in the saddlebags. The onions had been the last of her store, and the grain and flour were both low, while apparently enemies lay waiting in the woods all around them. He moved stiffly and tugged the blankets tighter around his shoulders, wondering what Cybelle was fleeing from and where she was flying to—but there was nothing he could do about it in any case. She would take him with her or leave him behind. And if she abandoned him, he would be lost, so he wouldn't press her.

The wail of the wind was lonely, like a host of damned souls crying through the trees. He fed the fire and nodded in the fluttering shadows. Toward midnight he waked her to take the second watch, and fell to sleep himself without being aware even that he lay down. Toward morning he heard the wind fall off, dimly, through sodden dreams.

The mare wakened him, shifting her feet too close to his head. Ta Nyahl lay for a while in the warmth of his blankets, feeling the chill bite his nose. He was wrapped in the wool like a cocoon, but he opened a flap over his eyes to have a look at the weather. It was almost daylight, and the snow was still falling heavily. The raging blizzard of the previous night was gone, though, so the immediate dangers were past. This was merely snow. Cybelle was sitting at the lip of the rock ledge, still wrapped in her blankets, watching the heavy flakes.

As Ta Nyahl stirred, the mare snorted, and Cybelle looked around.

"Are you awake?" she asked. "I was going to let you sleep."

He sat up, too, and pushed the mass of his hair out of his face, raked through the damp tangles with his fingers. He still ached with weakness and exhaustion this morning, but the bay whickered at him, wanting feed, and in a moment he got up and checked to see if his clothes were dry. The wool was only slightly damp this morning. He went behind the horses to put that on and pulled one of the blankets around his shoulders again like a cloak. The leather outer clothing was stiff and hard, and would need work before he wore it again. He left it where it lay by the fire, and measured out portions of grain for the horses. While the bay was eating, he checked down its legs for damage to see why it was limping, but found nothing. Checking the horse's hooves, he found what seemed to be a bruise on the frog of the right forefoot that was likely causing the problem. Continuous travel would be hard on it, and Ta Nyahl thought they should keep it in mind when setting the pace from now on.

When he was done with the horses, Cybelle had bread and gravy made from last nights' drippings for their breakfast. It wasn't much, and it might be nearly the last of their supplies, but it was filling and left a warmth in his belly that was encouraging. After they had eaten and cleaned up, Cybelle sat down to frown and watch it snow. When he began to search through the cooking supplies, she turned around.

"What are you doing?" she asked.

"The wet will damage the leather," he said. "If it suits you, lhassa, I will work on it."

She lifted her eyebrows.

"Please do," she said. "I thought it was ruined."

He thought the leather hadn't been well cared for in the first place or it would have shed water better, but he decided that saying anything about it might be an affront. He thought she had gotten the horses and gear from the headman at the village they had escaped two nights before, and certainly the man would not have given her his best to take away.

Ta Nyahl found the cooking fat and sat by the fire where the heat would warm the tallow. Then he rubbed it into the stiffened leather of both their clothes and the tack, working it with his hands and making it supple and dark—but also rubbing his scent into it, making it his so it didn't seem so alien any more. The woman made no objection to what he was doing with her things, but then humans didn't seem to be as aware of scent as the kria. Most likely she had no thoughts about it.

When he was working on his jacket, he found the fiber he had stuffed into his pocket yesterday. He still needed to finish the string, so he laid the wad of it aside until he was finished with the work on the leather. Then he sat by the fire again and began to work through the snarl of fibers. The beginnings of the braid he had made were good, and he continued, making it longer. As he worked, he rubbed the fat on his fingers into the twine to make it stronger and more waterproof.

When he got one length completed, he thankfully braided and bound back the mass of his hair with the twine. But string was useful for other things, as well. He immediately began work on another length, and then a third.

The sun made an invisible advance up the sky, and the wan light shifted inside their shelter. Ta Nyahl got up and put the last of the logs on the fire, checked the weather. The snowfall had lightened, and maybe soon it would be over. The woman continued to watch the snow, apparently lost in her own thoughts, and he was relieved to have her attention elsewhere. It meant he didn't have to endure the pressure of her eyes.

He went back to work. When he had the two lengths of string finished, he tied a loop in the end of one, and then hesitated, momentarily stymied, wondering what he could use for a pouch. A piece of the leather would be best, but he had nothing to cut it with. The blankets were the next best option, he decided, and after a moment of work with his teeth, he managed to tear a corner off the slightly ragged wool blanket he was using for a cloak. He fastened the lengths of string he had made securely to either side, and immediately felt better than he had since he had lost his kria-made weapons to the humans. It wasn't much, but he was armed again.

The woman had apparently missed what he was doing. She had refused him an adult's weapons, but this was a child's tool that was more appropriate for his status as a slave. He stood and tucked the sling into the pocket of his leather jacket, opposite the pocket full of river stones. His leather outer clothing was now warm and pliable with the tallow, and he laid aside the blanket cloak and pulled on the leather skirt and the jacket along with his boots. He went then and knelt by the woman, keeping his eyes downcast.

"Lhassa," he said. "The last of the wood is on the fire. If you will give me your axe again, I will bring more."

She got up and found the axe, handed it to him.

"Be careful," she said. "It looks like the drifts might be deep."

"Yes, lhassa," he said.

He went to saddle the mare, endured her wickedness with better patience than yesterday. His shoulder seemed to be healing, the infection gone. He could use his left arm a little today, which made it easier to lift the saddle into place and pull the girth tight. He thought the mare recognized him well enough now, but still she tried to bite. He had to watch her carefully.

When he was done with the saddle, he led her past Cybelle and down out of the fissure and into the snow. It came up to about mid-calf on the trail, but the woman was right that drifts would be much deeper. The snowfall seemed to have lightened for now, and the ground was a pristine and searing white. The snow lay thick on the branches of the trees and on the boughs of the evergreens. The air smelled clear and sharp. A yellow bird flitted across the trail ahead of them, disturbed by the click of the mare's hoof on a rock.

Snowflakes caught in his hair and his eyelashes, coated the newly oiled surface of his jacket. Without the wind, the temperature seemed barely cold enough to keep the snow on the ground, and he thought it would begin to melt as soon as the day warmed. The trees had already put on new leaves, and it was late for such a heavy snow in the valley. Perhaps by afternoon they could travel.

Ta Nyahl retraced his way to the fallen tree he had found the evening before and cut more of the branches, strapped them on the mare's back. It wasn't far back to the camp, and they quickly retraced their way to the rocky outcrop and the ledge.

The woman looked at him questioningly.

"How was the snow?" she asked. "Can we travel today?"

"Maybe," he said. "As the day warms, it will begin to melt, and there will be mud. We will leave a trail that's easy to follow."

She considered. "I guess I'll have to live with that," she said.

"Is there a village near where we could get more rations?" she asked. "I guess we could forage, but I'd rather trade some of the gear or blankets for flour and grain."

He plotted a route mentally. They had made progress toward the mountains, and they weren't very far from the foothills now, but it would still be a while before they began to come up out of the valley into steeper elevation.

"Yes, lhassa. There is a village to the west that we might pass by."

"What are the people like? Is it safe?"

He tried to work through the question. What was safe for her wouldn't necessarily be safe for him. In this case, he thought it wouldn't be safe for either of them. His choice would have been to continue with foraging and keep away from the villages, altogether.

"No, lhassa," he said truthfully. "I don't think so."

The sun came out suddenly in late morning. The temperature climbed sharply, turning the show wet and slushy. Snowmelt began to drip from the overhang above them. They loaded the horses and set off down the faint game trail. It took Ta Nyahl a little while to orient, as they had gone well off track in the storm. However, it was fairly easy to retrace the way they had come, and by noon he knew with certainty where they were headed.

Travel was slow because of the snow and mud, but they made good progress. If men were following them, Ta Nyahl hoped they wouldn't pick up the new trail. It was impossible not to leave tracks in the mud. The horses sank up to their fetlocks in some places. After a while he drew rein, as he could feel the mare struggling under him to lift her feet.

"What is it?" asked Cybelle.

"We need to stop for a while," he said. "The horses' feet are too heavy with the mud."

They stopped and he dug the packed mud out of their hooves with a sturdy stick that he managed to break into a point. The mare refused to lift her feet, and he had to lean into her to shift her balance, but the bay seemed grateful for the attention. He took care around the gelding's bruised frog. When he was done, he cleaned his hands in the remains of snow.

Cybelle had gotten out some bread leftover from breakfast for a mid-day meal, but he refused it.

"Do you still want to go to the village?" he asked.

"Yes," she said.

"Then, we will need this for tonight," he said. "We'll be too close to light a fire."

Cybelle had eaten part of her bread, but at that she stopped eating and wrapped it up again. She put it away in the saddlebag.

Twice more during the afternoon they stopped to clean the horses' feet. By late in the afternoon, the fairly even terrain of the valley had been replaced by gentle hills, and they started to see more evergreens. The ground grew drier as the elevation rose, and traveling became a little easier.

Ta Nyahl stayed off the trails, cutting through the open woods whenever possible. It worried him that Cybelle meant to stop and barter at a human village. It seemed a terrifying idea to ride up openly and call out to the villagers. It was something he would never have considered doing by himself. The very idea sent a shiver along his spine.

As the day waned, Ta Nyahl began to look for a secure place to camp, rejected two or three possible sites as too exposed. Finally, as dusk turned the forest a darker green, he had to choose, managed to find a pond well hidden by rocks and brush. He rubbed down the horses and cleaned their feet again—it wouldn't do if both of them went lame. Then he went into the forest to break evergreen boughs to keep the wet out of the blankets as they slept. He laid them on the ground and spread out the blankets.

Cybelle got out the last stores of cold bread that she had fried and stored in the pack. She also cut the last few parings of cheese. Ta Nyahl ate what she gave him, but he was still hungry when he was done.

"I've saved a little bread for a breakfast," she said, "but it's not much. Did you say the village is near here?"

"Yes," he said.

"How far?"

"We could be there by mid-morning," he said.

"What should I offer in trade?" she asked.

It was a curious question from a human woman. Again, it suggested she didn't know that much about the villages here—that she was working on alien ground. It mattered little, though. He had already decided she was no kin of the villagers.

He thought about the idea of trade. According to the elders, it had been many years since the kria had traded with humans, but still he knew what was important.

"They will want metal tools, lhassa," he said.

She went to the pile of tack and brought one of the saddlebags, took out two knives, a bone awl and some fishhooks.

"Will these do?"

"Yes," he said, counting up the value of the items. Besides these things, the headman in the last village had given her the horses and gear—and his kria captives. The man must have been terrified of her.

"I can't give all the knives away," she said. "But we need the supplies. I can keep the one I've been using and trade these two. How much in rations will these be worth?"

He thought about it. Metal tools were sought after in the villages, and the workmanship of these knives was at least fair—the steel was good and the edges were undamaged.

"If I were to trade these," he said, "I would expect at least two weeks of supplies."

"Alright," she said. "That's what I'll ask for, then."

She took the first watch, but he slept fitfully during his turn to sleep, disturbed by their nearness to the human village. There would be dangers early in the morning when they might easily be discovered by hunters going out before daylight. He stayed sharply alert during his watch, listening to every sound, checking the messages that the wind brought. When morning broke, he was fairly sure their camp had been undiscovered. He had chosen the placement well.

Chapter 6

Ta Nyahl was suffering from the cold by the time Cybelle stirred. The first light of dawn was filtering through the trees by then, turning the forest a misty pale and casting long shadows on the patchy snow. He tried moving his shoulder and found it was better again today. Still, working the stiffness out started a bone-deep ache.

They ate the last of the bread, and he used Cybelle's knife to cut some of the cattails that grew by the pond for breakfast. The insides of the stalks were edible, if not that easy to chew without cooking. It wasn't the kind of food he preferred, but it helped fill their bellies and would carry them through the morning.

They packed up their things and loaded the horses. By the time the sun's rays began to glint through the trees, they were mounted and on the way. The horses made steady progress, even though the terrain was noticeably steeper here. Their breaths made clouds of vapor in the early morning chill.

Ta Nyahl stirred in the saddle, restless and alert for any dangers. It seemed Cybelle was on edge, too.

"We're still on schedule to be there by mid-morning?" she asked.

"Yes," he said.

"Can we just ride into the village?" she asked.

He thought about it. The kria camps had sentries, and it would be impossible to come even this close without them knowing. That was important to make sure the actual camp wouldn't be discovered. There would be a warning of approaching strangers relayed back so the women and children could hide, or that the whole camp could disappear, if need be. They could pack up and move to a different site within just a short time, leaving only rough shelters and heaps of midden behind. If worst came to worst, they would leave their possessions and just go.

However, the human villages were more permanent. They cleared spaces around them and built palisades to protect against both animal and human marauders. If there was an alarm, the warriors defended the village through gaps between the logs. The palisades gave them a feeling of security, which meant they didn't have the same kind of sentry system as the kria. This had made it easy for the small band of Da Hanath, Da Kathan and Ta Nyahl to cause trouble for the human villages during the last year. With no far-flung sentries to detect them, they had been able to come right up to the village walls at night.

Visitors normally rode out of the woods and hailed the village, he knew, and waited to make sure they were welcome before riding further across the open space toward the village gates. By staying close to the woods, they could easily take cover from the archers if it turned out they were unwelcome. In this case, he would certainly be unwelcome. Word would surely have spread about his capture by the humans—they had to have known who he was.

"Lhassa," he said. "I cannot go into the village."

Her eyes flashed. "Then I'll ride in by myself."

He considered that. Normally it would be unsafe, as humans had little respect for women without protection. However, it was likely that her reputation as a witch had already spread through the human villages, too, at least the ones in this part of the forest. It was also likely that the villagers knew that she had taken him as a slave. Because of this, they might want to come out and see her with their own eyes, and they might offer a certain respect. It all depended on what tales had spread about her witchcraft.

"Not into the village," he said. "It won't be safe."

She looked at him, thought about it.

"Alright, then," she said. "I'll stay fairly close to the trees in case there's trouble. You can wait for me at the edge of the woods."

He led the way with more care as they approached the village—alert and silent, as if they were planning a raid. He caught the scents of it long before they were within sight of the palisade and the gates. The stink of humans and horses was unmistakable on the wind, and the smoke of the cook fires eddied and drifted, carrying messages for anyone who could read them.

Within the forest, the tall trees shaded out smaller brush and weeds, and traveling off the trail had been relatively easy. As they got closer to the edge of the woods, though, the brush would get thick enough that they would have to force their way through. In case they had to run, it would be best to avoid that.

Plus, Cybelle meant to hail the village. That meant they should come to the gates. Once he could hear sounds from the village, Ta Nyahl circled through the open woods to the trail. That made traveling easier and allowed them to approach the dwellings by the expected route. This added the danger that they might meet someone, but they didn't. They came safely to the edge of the trees and found the gates lying before them.

The palisade looked sturdy. It was built of vertical logs set into the ground and fastened together with ropes. The upper ends of the logs were sharpened to discourage anyone from climbing over. Above the palisade, the grass-thatched roofs of the huts were easily visible. The smoke of cook fires rose and drifted on the wind. The gates were open at this hour of the morning, and the trail widened slightly as it wove through the short spring grass toward the gates.

Ta Nyahl stopped, made one last check. Then he pulled the mare off to the side of the trail so the woman could ride past him and out into the open. She gave him a final glance, and he thought her face looked still and pale in the morning light. As she rode by, she slipped her hand into the pocket of her jacket where she kept the black object he had seen in her hand before.

He might not quite understand her relations with the villagers, but he expected she might do well in this trade. She had dealt well with the last village headman in bargaining for his own life. Still, there were a lot of uncertainties in the situation.

The woman rode about a span out of the woods, then pulled her horse to a stop.

"Hail the village!" she called in a clear voice.

It carried well enough. Ta Nyahl saw a flurry of sudden activity inside the gates at the shout from a stranger. His careful approach to the village had apparently taken them completely by surprise. Humans might have made a lot of noise on the trail, talking and moving carelessly, but caution and fading into the background were ingrained habits for the kria. He could have slipped away just as easily now—but that would have left Cybelle unprotected.

She had told him to wait by the woods, which put him at a safe distance from archers, but that meant she was taking on any dangers herself. The woman conducted herself with confidence, but he had seen the uncertainty in her eyes. He thought it wouldn't do for her to look alone. He needed to be seen.

He shuddered with something like panic at the idea. The mare shifted nervously under him and snorted, feeling his distress. He wanted to fade into the brush. Every instinct screamed that he should leave the woman and disappear. He was still grappling with his role as her slave, but still he knew that hiding wouldn't serve her well. Her reception depended on how seriously the village warriors took the rumors of her witchcraft. If it seemed she was protected by magic, then it followed that he was, too. He needed to let them know he believed that.

He straightened his back, lifted his chin and urged the mare out a little distance behind Cybelle, far enough that he would be clearly visible. He didn't want the open trail to his back where someone could come up on them, so he moved the horse off a little to the side of the trail. Here, he had brambles behind him and a clear line of sight to the village and the gates. He stopped the mare and waited.

"Who comes?" A warrior armed with a bow and spear stepped out into the center of the gates.

"Cybelle Lawton," the woman replied. "I've come to trade for supplies."

"To trade?" answered the warrior.

"Where is your headman?" she said. "I would speak directly with him."

The man looked past her at Ta Nyahl. He was dressed like a human in the leather clothing, but even over the distance it was probably clear what he was. The man looked back at Cybelle.

"Are you the witch?" he asked.

"I've been called that," said Cybelle. "I mean you no harm, though. I have goods to trade. I want to speak with your headman."

The man ducked back through the gates. There was a stir as he conferred with someone else, and then a delay. After a while the headman appeared. The warrior talked to him, and he looked out at Cybelle, then at Ta Nyahl.

"Witch," he called. "Why have you brought a kria to our village?"

"He is my servant," said Cybelle. "Will you trade with me?"

The man thought about it. "I will trade for the kria," he said.

"No," said Cybelle. "He's mine. I have metal tools that I will trade for supplies."

"For the kria," said the man.

"No," said Cybelle again. "Do you want the tools or not? I have knives."

The man thought about it, looked at Ta Nyahl again.

"I will come look at what you have," he said.

By now there was something of a crowd behind the palisade walls. Word had spread within the village of who had come to trade, and everyone there was trying to get a look. Ta Nyahl saw women and children in the crowd now, mixed with the warriors. He didn't like the way Cybelle's conversation with the headman had gone. He didn't like waiting there in front of the gates. His breath was coming faster, and tension had started to build along his back and shoulders. A quiver ran along his nerves. The mare tossed her head and pranced sideways in response. He touched the river stones in the pocket of his jacket, feeling their smooth texture.

The headman started out along the trail from the gates, backed up by two warriors. They covered the distance quickly enough, still watching Ta Nyahl as much as the woman. The men stopped in front of her.

"Headman," she said. "I am Cybelle Lawton. How should I address you?"

"I am Dirkin," he said.

They were no longer shouting, but Ta Nyahl's ears were quick enough to hear what they said. The man was stocky and dark skinned, with a flat nose and flaring ears. His belly stuck out over the band of his trousers, strained against the woolen shirt he wore. It spread the opening of his leather jacket. The warriors were dark, as well, but they looked more able.

"Well met, Headman Dirkin," Cybelle said. She didn't get off the horse. "Here is what I have to trade."

She had the items wrapped in an oiled cloth, opened the folds of it to show what she had.

"Let me have them," said Dirkin. "I need to feel the edge on the knives."

"Bring the supplies first," she said. "I need enough for two weeks of rations for myself and my servant, feed for the horses."

The headman looked at the knives again, nodded to one of the warriors. The man turned and trotted back to the village. Apparently they thought the deal was good enough. Cybelle was a canny trader, and it seemed to be going well. Ta Nyahl drew an easier breath, but his heart was still beating hard in his throat.

They carried out the supplies in fiber baskets, set them on the ground in front of Cybelle. There was talk from the village folk now, a faint ripple of conversation from the distance. The warriors waiting with the headman shuffled their feet and whispered to each other, watching the woman.

"Empty them out," Cybelle said. "I need to see what's there."

They turned over the containers, and the goods spilled out. The baskets had been full, with no attempt to cheat at the trade. It looked to be smoked meat, fat, flour, salt, grain, tubers and cheese—a generous supply.

"Good," said Cybelle. "That's sufficient. Here are the tools. I'm sure you'll find them good enough."

She had been holding them on the pommel of her saddle, still wrapped, but now she lifted the bundle and held it out to the headman. He stepped up to take it, caught hold of her wrist instead.

Ta Nyahl saw her sway in the saddle. He had almost seen the intent in the headman's stride. The sling was already in his hands. He spun it once and let fly.

The stone clipped the headman's ear. He let go of Cybelle like she was made of hot coals, jumped backward. He snapped his head around to look at Ta Nyahl, reached up to touch his ear. The stone had cut him—a trickle of blood ran down his neck.

The warriors shifted, put hands on their weapons. The move had been quick enough that they had missed it, but they knew where the stone had come from. The mare jerked her head and snorted. Ta Nyahl tightened the reins to keep her still, kept his chin up and looked straight back at them. The yellow in his eyes must have been clear—they were barely a span away.

"Thank you for the trade," said Cybelle. "Perhaps we'll meet again, headman."

Her voice was cold this time. The man looked back at her, again at Ta Nyahl. They were within arrow flight. If given the word, the warriors could have shot him and Cybelle both— but the invisible threat of witchcraft was still there, hanging over the trade. It might be an uncertain threat, but Cybelle had her hand in the pocket of her jacket. Ta Nyahl thought it was very real.

The headman decided against testing her sorcery.

"Well met, Cybelle Lawton," he said. "Yes. Perhaps we can trade again some other time."

The men backed up, turned and headed back to the village. They walked steadily back, as if everything was perfectly fine, but now and then one of the warriors turned and looked back to make sure there was no hex following after them. The crowd parted at the gates to let the headman pass. The distant murmur of conversation increased. Somewhere a child cried.

Once the men were completely back within the gates, Cybelle turned in the saddle and looked back at Ta Nyahl.

"Help me load the supplies," she said. She sounded angry.

He twitched the mare's reins and rode forward. She dismounted, started toward the goods.

"Lhassa," he said softly. "Let me do it."

She looked at him.

"Alright," she said. She stepped forward and glanced over the supplies, then moved back out of the way and waited while he portioned them out and added them to the packs on the backs of the saddles. He worked efficiently, unhappy with their exposed position. By now someone in the village could easily have gone over the palisade and come up behind them on the trail. He could only hope the threat of witchcraft would prevent the idea.

"It's done," he said, finally.

Cybelle turned from where she had been idly watching the crowd still at the gates. He held the bay's head while she mounted, then swung up on the mare with nearly his usual grace and strength. He thought he might pay for it later, but the pounding of his heart and the rush of blood in his veins hadn't slowed, even when the men had gone.

They had killed Da Hanath first because he was older, and they thought he was the cause of their troubles, but they had been mistaken. It was Ta Nyahl who carried the dishonor for leading his older cousins to their deaths. Because he belonged to Cybelle now, he would have to give up the path he had followed, but still the anger that had driven him was there underneath. He knew now that it was.

He let the woman lead off up the trail. As soon as they were past the overgrowth of brush, he said quietly, "Here, lhassa."

She stopped the bay and looked back, and he turned the mare off the trail and into the open woods. She urged her horse in behind him.

As they rode, he tested the wind currents, wary of anyone who might be waiting for them in the woods or following behind on their trail. A breeze normally blew from the direction of the sea and turned in the afternoon. The air was fairly still this late in the morning. He arranged the direction of their travel so it would bring the most information, stayed alert for any unusual sounds. There seemed no pursuit from the village.

They moved swiftly, and by noon were well away from the settlement. Ta Nyahl felt confident enough to stop at a little spring to fill their water skins and rest the horses. They dismounted, and he slipped the horses' bits to let them drink.

By the time he was done with the horses, Cybelle had unpacked some of the cattails he had cut in the morning and some cheese.

"Here," she said, handing a share to him.

The warmth in his blood had gone by then, and had left him weak and lightheaded. He took the food in unsteady hands, sat down carefully on a low rock to eat. The woman sat on a fallen log.

"Thank you," she said.

He had been peeling the leaf covering off a cattail stem to expose the starchy flesh beneath, but now he stopped.

"For what, lhassa?"

"That was you with the stone, wasn't it?"

He risked a quick glance at her face, dropped his eyes again. He had interfered with her trading when she had told him to wait. Plus, he had made the sling in direct defiance of her refusal of weapons. He knew she must be annoyed, but her face only looked ordinary, as if she were fully absorbed in peeling the stems, herself.

When he didn't answer, she went on. "It went close enough to my head that I felt the wind off it."

He felt his face burn at that. He had risked her safety, after all. His aim could have been off through lack of practice with the weapon, or his injuries might have betrayed him. If the stone had been just a hand's breath to the left, it would have struck her instead of the headman. At the time, he hadn't thought of it, though. He had only acted—and his aim had been true.

"I thought there was going to be trouble," she said, "but that stopped it. I just wanted to say thank you."

His continued silence was awkward. The thanks required a respectful response, but answering would require admitting to the deed.

"Yes, lhassa," he said, but stuck at that. He wasn't sure what else to say about it.

"It was a good shot," she said casually. "Where did you get the stone?"

"From the creek," he said finally.

"Ah," she said. "And how did you launch it?"

"A sling, lhassa," he said.

"Where did you get it?" she asked. "Did you make it?"

"Yes," he said. "It's only a little bit of twine."

He thought she would say more, but she didn't. He risked another glance, found she had only tightened her lips at the revelation.

She bit down on a piece of cheese, went on in a matter-of-fact tone. "Did you hear what the headman said?" she asked. "He wanted to trade for you."

He dropped his head, afraid for her to see the shame and anger that must have flooded his eyes. He took a breath.

"Yes, lhassa," he said. "I heard."

His voice was quiet and even, gave away nothing.

"Why?" she asked.

He debated an answer. Relations between the humans and the kria were generally bad, but the humans had special reasons for wanting to be rid of him, personally. If she didn't know about that, it wasn't something he wanted to tell her. Once she had heard the whole story, there was a danger that she might do as she had suggested before and reject the oath he had sworn to her—maybe send him back to the villagers. The shame of this situation was bad enough, but that would leave him with nothing.

He had thought for a moment when he heard it that she would consider the trade. After all, she could probably exchange him for safe passage to wherever she wanted to go, along with at least a month's rations and several knives. Still, she seemed to distrust the villagers, herself—maybe even more than she distrusted him. He thought he'd best be careful what he told her.

"Humans hate the kria," he said, finally.

"So they wanted to finish the job the other village started?"

"Yes," he said. He picked at the cattail in his hands, shredding the leaf wrapping. He had been hungry, but now his stomach was filled with acid.

"So why do they hate your people?" she asked. "Is there a war going on?"

"Not on the side of the kria," he said. He thought this was part of the problem in relations with humans—the war was all on one side.

"Well, that's nice to hear," she said.

She was done with her meal, brushed the crumbs and litter off her lap.

"I'm sorry," she said then, seeing that he hadn't eaten. "I've spoiled your lunch with the questions."

Ta Nyahl held the rations in his hands a moment longer, but his taste for them was gone now. He finally tucked them into a pocket to eat later on. The woman pulled the water skins from the spring, pushed in the stoppers. He took them and went to see to the horses, to make sure they didn't drink too much. He loaded the water skins and tightened the girths to the saddles.

As he tugged at the straps, he caught the scent of humans on the wind. He stopped and lifted his head, seeking for a better acuity. He had almost expected that someone from the village would follow them, had ridden with the wind at their backs since they had left it to make sure he was aware if they did. This wasn't village scent, though.

The village had had a particular stink—of wood smoke and stale grease, the musky scent of the huts. This was different. He realized now that he had caught this scent before when they had hidden from the men at the river crossing. Their clothing held a different odor, and they carried a lot of metal—this scent had an edge of steel.

"What is it?" asked Cybelle.

She was standing beside him now, studying his distraction.

"Human men," he said, "on our back trail."

"From the village?" she asked.

He hesitated. "No," he decided finally. "From somewhere else. It may be the men who were following you before."

"Damn," she said. "I'd hoped…" She stopped. "How far back?"

He tried to calculate the distance.

"This side of the village," he said, "but not too far past it. They may know we stopped there."

"Let's go," she said. "We need to stay ahead of them."

She caught up the bay's reins, pulled up into the saddle. Ta Nyahl cleaned up the debris left from their meal, quickly tried to erase their sign from the clearing. Then he mounted the mare and led off.

He zigzagged back and forth across the wind, keeping in touch with messages from behind them. They made good time, regardless. The afternoon was almost warm, and the ground was drying out from the snowmelt. The terrain had shifted, and it was clear they had entered the foothills to the mountains. Once or twice they dismounted to walk up a steep incline, resting the horses. The breeze shifted direction in the afternoon, cutting off most of the information about the men following them, but Ta Nyahl expected they could stay ahead through steady travel. He took pains to hide their sign whenever possible, saved the horses' strength for when they might need it.

At mid-afternoon, he thought he caught scent from the south. He turned quarter wind, wondering if the group of men had divided and circled. There had been eight at the stream crossing, and there may have been more that he hadn't seen. The shadows were growing long when they topped a rise, and he caught human scent ahead of them. He mare shied at his sudden fright. He tightened the reins, turned to look behind them again.

"What's wrong?" asked Cybelle.

"Trouble," he breathed. "Lhassa, we are surrounded by human men."

"Surrounded?" she echoed.

"Yes," he said "They're in front of us, too." He looked at her, found her face full of concern, but not panic, as yet. She had steady nerves.

"Dammit," she said.

There was something worrying about the way the men had closed on them, as if they knew where to move and where to cut him off. It felt like sorcery—a shiver ran along his spine at the thought. He found a fragment of memory—the shaman in the human village that killed Da Hanath and Da Kathan had bragged that he could find the kria by his magic. Perhaps witchcraft was something he should take seriously.

"Is there a way out?" Cybelle asked.

He let out his breath. "It will be hard to hide the horses," he said. "We have choices. We can leave them and try to get away on foot; we can meet the men and you can talk with them, or we try to slip past."

She heaved out a sigh.

"Great. I don't want to talk with them," she said. She put her hand in her pocket, touching the dark object he had glimpsed before. "Can we get past?"

"I don't know, lhassa," he said.

He thought about it. He was traveling now with someone the villagers thought was a witch. Perhaps the men would be cautious, too, hold back just enough that they could slip through.

"They seem to know where we are and where we're headed. If we turn off our path for a while we might slip past them," he said.

"Alright," she said quietly. "Let's go."

He doubled back, stopping often to check the wind and moving north by instinct into rougher terrain. They worked their way through thickets and over rocky slopes, waded through streams to hide their sign. Everything seemed clear, but he knew the men were still there, closing up the distance. He wondered again why the woman was fleeing from them. She seemed to think it was her business and not his, but he was beginning to think he should ask if she knew about their sorcery. He tried to analyze it as they rode.

The existence of this kind of magic was something that hadn't impressed him before. It had seemed odd the way he and Da Hanath had been captured and Da Kathan killed. He had thought it was only an unhappy accident that the humans had happened on them in the woods. But if there was sorcery at work, maybe it hadn't been so much an accident, after all.

This seemed to be something similar. He and Cybelle had certainly lost the men during the storm, but now they seemed to know exactly where to look for the two of them.

Was it possible they knew Cybelle was headed toward the mountains, had set a trap on the route to the pass? Or was it possible that the people in the village where they had traded in the morning had some way to communicate with the hunters? He had heard tales of sorcerers who could see the future in dreams or in still water. He had also heard of humans using trained messenger birds to carry warnings. Whatever, it was clear that these men knew where to look for Cybelle. The question was whether they had only made an accurate guess, or whether they were aided by something supernatural. He shivered at the idea—the intimation of things he didn't understand.

The woods were growing dusky by the time he called a halt. He had been hoping the men would pass by them to the south and be well out of the way by now, but they seemed to have tarried instead. Whatever, the problem hadn't resolved itself. Still, the men seemed to be headed in the wrong direction now, and he thought he and Cybelle would have a chance to slip by without being seen during the darkness.

"They are mainly south of us now," he told her. "If we continue north, then I think we can ride past them in the night."

They stopped to eat a cold evening meal, then tightened the saddle girths and set off again as the clouds colored with sunset. The first moon wouldn't rise until later. Cybelle might have a hard time navigating in the darkness, but he would be able see well enough. He meant to continue on to the north, but had to turn back south within a little while when they ran into a rocky escarpment that blocked their route. Unless the men did have some kind of sorcery, he thought he must have evaded them.

He had made a mistake, though. They climbed a low hill, and the wind eddied suddenly, brought the scent of humans already too close—turbulence around the escarpment had hidden their scent. He pulled the mare to a stop and jerked around to warn Cybelle. He was too late—the bay had already whickered.

Cybelle had seen him turn. The look on her face was questioning, but then a voice shouted off to the right. A group of men rode out from behind a grove of trees, already on top of them.

There was nothing to do but run.

Their horses were tired, but so were those of the pursuers. They had passed an area of heavy undergrowth only a short distance back. If they could make it into the brush, they might disappear. Ta Nyahl urged the mare into a gallop, looked back to make sure the woman was with him. The horses skidded back down the hill. Momentum carried them up the other side. The next hill was steeper, and Ta Nyahl set the horses at it—already seeing the canes that could be their salvation.

Chapter 7

The mare surged upward, topped the hill, and then he became aware that the bay horse wasn't beside him. He dragged the mare's rush to a stop, feeling her sides heave under him. He caught sight of the gelding off to the right— but without a rider. He swung desperately around in the saddle then to search down the hill. The mare fought him, sidestepped and sawed her jaw against the reins. Foam flew from the bit as she tossed her head.

Horsemen were already crashing through the brush within earshot, on the other side of the hollow. There was no time to think about what to do. He slid out of the saddle, looped the reins over the saddle horn and slapped the mare on the hindquarters. Perversely she tried to bite him then, but he shoved her head away so that she shied back instead, ran off through the trees. He whirled and lunged back down the hill. It was completely reckless. Even if they didn't see him sliding down, he would leave deep tracks gouged into the loam. But the ground was already torn up by the horse's assent. Maybe no one would be able to sort out the different prints in the poor light to see which way he had gone. Maybe he could find cover quickly enough at the bottom. Sinkingly, he thought not.

He was sure the lame gelding had fallen and thrown his rider. The wind had turned, wasn't any help to him now. As he ran, he had to search along the path they had ridden with only his eyes. His legs ached with the speed. He was gasping for breath by the time he reached the bottom of the hill. He pressed his elbow to his ribs where a stitch jabbed at him and kept running. Rocks jutted from the soil, a danger the mare had evaded. Fallen timber cut the slopes with rotting, mossy shadows. He tried to line up the path the horses had taken, ran through the damp remains of last year's leaves, increasingly conscious that he hadn't so much as a knife to protect himself. He would die if he were caught here.

He found the woman just as the first of their pursuers broke into the open on the rim—a still, dark form in the shade of a partially fallen tree. He slid flat beside her in one final plunge, regardless of how that hurt, rolled her over beneath the log and fell across her. Then he froze, holding back his pain and trying not to smother as he struggled to get a grip on his panting. He had gone to ground right under the noses of the horsemen—couldn't believe they hadn't seen him, even in the dusk. He lay like the dead.

They crashed down the hill, shouted as they caught sight of the gelding, still halfway up the hill. They actually galloped their horses past where he hid, smothering under the log. He wondered at their blindness, but he could see better in the dusk than humans could. Maybe that was why they had missed him. Or maybe they confused one another with their excitement. Now half of them thundered off after the bay, and the others milled around in the floor of the hollow, obliterating the very tracks that would have given away his position. He controlled his gasping with an effort, drew breath carefully under cover of the noise they made, letting his heart slow gradually.

The bay gelding had bolted immediately, and the men who gave chase failed to catch him. They began to search the hollow instead for his missing rider, casting back and forth, shouting and trotting the horses as the light failed and the shadows grew darker. The brown leather of Ta Nyahl's boots and clothing faded into the earth, and he waited patiently, made no sudden starts to attract their eyes, however close they came. He lay still, listening to their talk, slightly different from what he was used to hearing. Three of them actually stopped within a span of him, angrily discussing what they should do, and still didn't see him lying beneath the log. He only waited for them to go away, easier now and lying quiet as the earth itself. Then Cybelle moved beneath him.

It was the worst possible moment for her to wake. He lay half on her, protecting her pale skin from the unfriendly eyes, but he couldn't hold her there. If she failed to realize the situation and panicked, if she made any sound or struggled beneath him—they were done. He was terrified by the idea, ran a quick calculation of their chance of running away from here, but the answer was—none. Desperately he moved one hand, soft as the lick of a flame, and laid it across her face instead, lightly against her mouth.

Her eyes came open then and she sucked in a breath to scream, but she must have recognized his scent or the texture of his hair that spilled over her face—or maybe his terror. Her eyes shifted and her breath caught, but she didn't scream. He felt her heart jump and labor, but she didn't move. She lay there still and controlled, listening as he did to the thud of horses' hooves, and the echoing of men's harsh voices nearby, growing more disgruntled as both light and search failed together.

He thought the men would go on somewhere else, but annoyingly, they decided to camp in the hollow, dry though it was. They did withdraw a distance in the direction the gelding had gone, maybe thinking the missing rider would attempt to go after the horse, or if both had escaped on one animal, that they could easily pick up the trail from there in the morning. They unsaddled their horses and built a fire as dark fell completely. As the glare of it rose, Ta Nyahl breathed more easily, dared to shift slightly and turn his head so his mouth lay against Cybelle's ear.

"Are you hurt, lhassa?" he asked.

"Dammit," she hissed. "Get off me."

He supposed that meant "no." He shifted over carefully to remove his weight from her, and she twitched immediately to get up. He grabbed at her, caught her wrist.

"Let go," she said, jerking against his grip.

"No," he breathed, and pushed her back down, pressing against her with his arm and one knee. When that didn't work, he slid completely over her again. "No," he warned. "Be still. They will hear, lhassa."

She twisted, and he thought she would struggle again, but she only breathed faster, lying quiet beneath him.

"We can't just stay here," she said.

"Yes," he insisted. "For a while."

She felt very slight under him, and completely rigid. He could feel the rebellion in every line of her body, and her breath gusted out in horror.

"Please, lhassa," he said against her ear, gripping her wrists. "Only until they sleep."

She lay tense, still mutinous but blessedly quiet, as if she understood the sense in what he wanted. He eased his grip on her then, assured that she would wait. Finally relaxing himself, he shifted again, hoping to find an easier position for his sore shoulder, but that seemed hopeless. It throbbed from the ill treatment, and there wouldn't be any help for it tonight. He sighed and lay still again, listening to what the human men were doing. There was still a great deal of moving around. A desultory murmur of argument crossed the hollow along with the rank cloud of their cooking. Now and then their horses shifted. What wind entered the cleft was blowing toward him, and he prayed to his predecessors that it wouldn't change to bring their scent to the animals. They would react to his scent at least, if not the woman's.

She seemed very warm. It was moldy and damp on the ground in this place the sun never reached, and the cold entered his bones and made his wounds ache, healing though most of them were. He was glad there was no frost tonight, and it seemed good to have a body next to him in the cold, regardless that it was a human's. Her warmth kept him from shivering. Her hair tickled his face as he breathed so that finally he raised a hand to brush at it. He felt her start at his touch and wondered if she had been dozing, but he thought not. She was still taut and completely awake as far as he could tell, not waiting with any ease of spirit. He was more adept at it than she. It would be a while before the men slept deeply enough for them to risk an escape, so he settled himself as comfortably as he could and began to doze.

Cybelle's scent kept company to his dreams. Oddly, it didn't seem offensive to him tonight, only faintly alien and comfortable and very female. He'd thought the time would never come when human scent would become bearable to him, much less pleasant. But she had grown familiar in the days they'd been together, and associated with tolerance if not with kindness. That had been a surprise. So now her closeness wasn't unpleasant, at least. After a while, he began to wonder belatedly why he had reacted so quickly above on the rim, when he had found she wasn't riding beside him any longer.

It was loyalty, he decided, working through it. And heartfelt—he hadn't even hesitated. Loyalty was something he had learned for his own people, for the clans of the kria, but this was someone different. This was a human woman to whom he was bound by an oath that he had given unwillingly, at the least, to save what he could from the ruin he had fallen into. But it seemed that his swearing to her wasn't such a burden. He wasn't so terrified of what she would do to him, didn't consider any longer that she was a witch sent to torment him. She seemed only a female, alien as she might be, and perhaps this oath was all that he had left of his life, all that was standing between himself and emptiness. So he had need of her now.

He sighed and opened his eyes to faint starlight. The camp was quiet. The second moon had set, leaving the hollow as dark as it would ever be. He gripped Cybelle's wrist and felt her move, tensing in response as if she had been lying awake all the time, only waiting for his signal. Assured that she was ready, he slid out from beneath the log, glanced at the camp slightly above them on the hill, careful to keep his eyes indirect so the green shine of them wouldn't catch the firelight. The flames had long since burnt down to coals. He identified a single sentry off to the side, not far enough from the light to be hidden. The fire glow outlined him clearly for one with the eyesight to make him out, a clear target for an assassin. But then, the man was only planning to foil human eyes. It was a typical mistake where kria were concerned.

Cybelle was working her way out from under the log stiffly, and he decided she must be bruised, at least, by the fall. Still, it was lucky she wasn't hurt worse, considering the roughness of the terrain and the proportion of rock surface to soft ground here. When she had straightened painfully, he took hold of her sleeve and tugged gently. She turned to follow, and he started back up the hill along the way he had come down, hoping again to hide their tracks in the torn ground the horses had left behind them. She slipped on dew-wet leaves and nearly fell, clutched at his forearm sharply.

"Dammit," she whispered.

He only hissed at her softly, meaning that she should be quiet, and after that she was. She didn't let go of his arm.

They had almost made it to the rim when an animal stirred in the thicket above them. A deer had come along the trail and scented them suddenly. It crashed away through the brush with the clear noise of a startled animal. Ta Nyahl ducked immediately, pulling the woman down with him. Below them, he could see the sentry straighten to alertness.

It wouldn't do for him to come investigate the noise. There had to be some reason for the deer to run.

He tucked his chin and expanded his chest, faked the coughing roar of a las bear. The woman beside him started and sucked in her breath at the sound. It was a good imitation, enough to bring a shiver along the nerves, and it would halt any plans the sentry had to investigate. Below in the hollow, the man checked to make sure his weapons were ready. One or two of the sleepers stirred, and one sat up. A murmur of voices rose, but no one came to check.

In a few more minutes, the hollow was quiet again. Ta Nyahl tugged at the woman's sleeve, and they continued the ascent. Once they were over the crest of the hill, he felt they were fairly safe. They only had to stay away from the men now until they went off to search for the horses.

As the third and final moon rose, he found a place to leave Cybelle, a hillside clothed in the sharp scent of loggerberry. The bushes would provide some cover, and the early berries would take care of minor hunger and thirst problems, at least until he could get back with something more substantial— or maybe with just the knowledge they would have to do without horses and supplies for a while. He would rather find the horses. Cybelle would find out for herself that the tart fruit was new and unripe, but it was the best he could do on short notice and in the dark.

"Stay here, please," he said.

"Where are you going?" she demanded, only a black shade now between him and the stars.

"I'm going to find the horses," he said.

"In the dark?"

"Yes," he said, wondering at her exasperation. "Better now than in the morning when the others will be looking, too."

She sat down suddenly at his feet. "A good point," she said. "Never mind."

He waited uncertainly, decided he had been dismissed. "There are berries, but beware the thorns," he said, and turned to go.

"When will you come back?" she asked.

He stopped. "I don't know, lhassa."

"By tomorrow night," she said. "Whether you've found them or not."

"Alright."

"Be careful," she said then. It was unexpected, and her voice sounded strange. He looked back at her, wondering what she meant, but her face was still in shadow and he couldn't read it. He decided that she didn't like the idea of being left alone in the dark.

"Yes, lhassa," he said. Then he started down the hillside, tracing his way back the way they had come.

He made a wide circuit around the hollow and cut an angle east on the other side to cross the horses' paths. He found the mare's first without any difficulty. She had left noxious droppings behind that he could scent even from a distance. Then too, he knew what direction she had started. The last moon of the night gave off little more light than the stars, but he was moving into what wind there was. The horse had passed recently enough that her scent still clung to the undergrowth. He had only to follow his nose and watch that he didn't step into anything nasty. Still it took a long time to find her, and even longer to catch her. She trotted away as soon as she saw him, nervous and quickly out of reach.

He stalked her quietly from downwind, made a rush, and she bolted with a snort and a kick, though she knew very well who he was and what he wanted. He followed, trying to control his irritation, knowing she would be aware of it and become even more perverse as his temper heated up. She had him indelibly cataloged as a predator.

Finally he managed to drive her into a blind gully and to trap her at the end. She tried to make a rush past him as he closed in. He strained his sore shoulder with the jerk it took to catch and hold her. Then she laid back her ears and tried to bite and kick, but he evaded that, and finally she succumbed to his authority, though with ill grace.

He mounted the cranky horse then, and began the weary ride back to cast for the gelding's trail. It was getting too near to morning for comfort, and he was leery of approaching the camp. Too late, he thought that with less knowledge of directions he should have looked for the gelding first. But he decided wearily that perhaps it was right this way after all. He was so tired he ached all over. He'd have hated to chase the mare in broad daylight when she could see that much better to escape from him.

He didn't trust the mare near the humans' horses. He left her tied a good distance away, went to investigate carefully on foot. The gelding's trail was completely obliterated near the camp by the cavalcade that had run over it, but he followed the torn track through the wood, found the place where they had veered in the wrong direction about a quarter length southwest. He thought about what to do then, and decided it would be safer to go after the mare, though he was tempted to follow the gelding now. Better to have one horse in hand at least. But the gelding had been running unevenly here, even more so than he had been before. Perhaps he would be too lame now to be ridden, which would mean an uncertain delay. Ta Nyahl cut through the trees then, began the long hike to where he had left the mare. His boots were beginning to rub, and he limped himself after a while.

Clearly the hard leather of these boots wasn't meant for walking. He wished again for his own worn, softer ones.

It was nearly an hour before he'd returned to cross the gelding's scent on horseback. The fast little moon was at zenith by then, and the sky was beginning to pale. He was fearful that the humans would have gotten an early start and passed him, already on the horse's trail, but there wasn't any sign of it, nor did he meet them at once. The wind had been quiet, but now it was shifting with the dawn, fluttering through the trees and washing clean the night's scents. Sight came with the sun, and he could track the horse almost as well that way, watching for the telltale signs that a hoof had pressed against soft mold here, unearthed a stone there, crushed fern under the trees further on. The gelding had left off running quickly, and hadn't gone far after that. He was grateful to find the horse so quickly, and seemingly in one piece. This one was friendlier, and made only a token resistance to being caught.

He got off the mare and ran his hands down its legs, decided all of them were sound, at least. There was still only the bruise on the frog of the right fore-hoof, though the horse must be sore from his fall. He had stepped on one of the reins and broken it, and the saddle was askew. Once caught, he seemed actually glad to see Ta Nyahl, and snuffed and nickered as if he expected to be fed and rubbed down now.

But it was too early for any of them to rest. Ta Nyahl found himself asleep once, loose in the saddle and at the mare's mercy in the midst of making a wide circle back toward the loggerberry hill. As the sun rose higher, he forced himself to alertness, knowing it would never do to be followed, and to have the human men find Cybelle through his carelessness. It would be as bad to be captured himself. He'd lose the horses, as well as maybe his life, and leave her stranded with nothing. It was best not to sleep on this horse, anyway. He sighed and straightened his back as the mare tried to scrape him against a tree, and twitched her head back toward open woods. The gelding limped tiredly along behind them.

It was nearly midday when he neared the hillside, and he made one final cast backward, looping behind to check his own trail. No one else had passed anywhere near. If he was followed, it wasn't aggressively. Perhaps he had slipped cleanly past the humans after all.

He approached the hillside carefully, afraid to startle the woman, and saw nothing out of order at first. But the horses had made enough noise that she would have heard and looked out to identify him. She didn't appear.

"Lhassa?" he called, hoping she was only asleep.

But she wasn't. She was gone.

It was a disaster he hadn't planned for. His urgency grew as he searched for her. He circled the hill, crossed the faint tracks he had made himself coming and going, and then found others further east. His lips tightened and pulled back as he saw them and caught the lingering scents—human men on horses. He glanced around sharply then. He had already checked and found nothing, but that wasn't assurance that they were gone. There was no fresh scent on the wind, no sounds but the shriek of distant kelbirds. He needed more information. He quelled his immediate impulses, left the horses tied in the concealment of the brush, and cautiously followed the tracks on foot back into the berry vines.

There had been two men. Two horses. They had left their stink clearly behind. He found Cybelle's track. She had been running, from the bite of the boot toe and the lightness of the heel. Then there was a place torn up from a struggle. They'd caught sight of her somehow and chased her here. The place stank of death and injury. Sitting on one heel, he shuddered at the reek of burnt flesh that hung in the air. It plunged him into memories of cruelty and torture, still too vivid, and of Da Hanath. His teeth appeared again in a half snarl, but he pushed down the anger that the visions brought him, and scrubbed his hands roughly across his face. He wished desperately that he weren't so exhausted—that he could think clearly what to do. There wouldn't be time for rest. He'd have to set off after them now—immediately—if he were to catch up in any reasonable time. But still the burnt odor disturbed him. He didn't want to leave without discovering the cause. He began to cast around the clearing, looking for other sign.

He found the weapon half under a swath of last year's leaves and trampled grass, but he didn't touch it at first. He recognized it, had seen it in Cybelle's hand in clear daylight, though the glimpse he'd had was quick. It was alien for certain, of metal and something else smooth and dark. It was the most curious thing about Cybelle, the thing that had made him realize at first what she must be. Human witches or ayeen wouldn't have any use for something like this, while a real women, alone and unprotected, would. And of course now he had a better idea what it did.

He picked it up finally, gently, the way he had seen her hold it, knowing it must be ready to work. There were knobs and levers coded in colors, but he was afraid to touch them, alien as the thing was. If he couldn't find her, maybe he would experiment with it later, but not now. He wrapped it carefully in oiled cloth and stored it in the gelding's saddlebags, insulated by the wrappings against any jostling that might set it off. There seemed to be nothing else to be read, except that the human scents here didn't match any of the group that had charged them last night. Instead, these were villagers. Was it random hunters then, who had happened on her by accident? He cursed to himself at the ill luck.

He hissed out a sigh then, decided that the horses needed care before he went anywhere. Cybelle would be abused, but probably not killed outright because she was a woman, and once her fangs were pulled—that being the black weapon— she might be useful to the human men in the way of other women. Still, if she had hurt one of them, they would be angry, and there might be consequences. He would have to be quick, whatever the case. Men on horseback could reach the nearby human village from here within a day, and once she was there, he could do little to get her back, unarmed and alone as he was. It was a dangerous chore even to attempt her rescue so near a human village. He would have no time to rest, himself, and no time to plan. But still he didn't hesitate, or even wonder why he didn't. If they traveled into the night, he had lost her. He could only follow and hope they gave him an opportunity.

He saw to the horses hurriedly, loosened the girths and fed them, gave each a container of water. There was grass in the clearings between the berry thickets, and he let the animals graze briefly while he ate cold meat and cheese, but he tasted nothing, chafing at the delay.

The mare was openly rebellious at leaving again so soon, blew up her ribs so he had trouble tightening the girth. He kneed her impatiently in the belly to make her exhale and as she grunted, he jerked at the straps. The usually compliant bay even limped sideways away from him. He was exhausted and starting a headache himself, and he had little sympathy, only a dull anger beginning that pounded along his nerves.

The track didn't go along the game trail, but set off in an erratic path through the woods. Still, the marks of the horses' hooves were easy enough to follow visually. He made fast progress, regardless of his own tired horses. He tried to save their strength, dismounting from the mare to walk up the steeper slopes himself. The day was chilly, and a fine, cold rain began to spit by mid-afternoon. His shoulder hurt, and as the mare slipped on a clump of wet leaves and jerked at the reins, pain ran up his neck and down his arm. He had hurt it the night before, and now it had stiffened up again.

He took a break to eat something and feed the horses as the sun set. The rain had stopped by then and a chill wind had started from the east. The horses turned their tails into it.

Chapter 8

Ta Nyahl kept going after dark, irritated by the slower progress, walking now and leading the horses. They dragged at the reins, unwilling and exhausted, and his blistered feet hurt with a painful rawness. The breeze that rose with nightfall blew odors away from him. Still, dismounted and close to the ground, he could track the humans by scent through the brighter darkness of the moonlight. The scent spoor was fresher here, and as the stars turned toward midnight, he began to grow concerned about what he was doing. A time estimate put them four hours ahead when he had begun tracking, and if they had stopped at dusk, he could be getting close without knowing it. Worse, he was moving upwind so they could catch his scent. Instinct stabbed at him. If these were kria, he would be moving into a trap for certain; that they weren't gave him little solace. He stopped the horses with his nostrils quivering uselessly. He had been praying the wind would turn, but it hadn't. Now he would have to make a decision.

He could keep going as he was and blunder onto their camp or maybe let them ambush him, or he could do something else. They had been traveling generally east in the direction of the human village, but on the same erratic, irritating, zigzag course that left him uncertain of their exact path. He could take a chance on gauging their direction and circle and come up from the east. But if he missed and lost the track, Cybelle was lost. He would face the infinitely harder task of getting her out of a defended village. He tried again to organize his scattered thoughts, to think what to do, and the mare shied at something and tossed her head, struck him in the jaw with her nose. Tears of pain filled his eyes, and he shook with sudden fury. He managed not to strike her and only cursed at the horse. Really it was humans that he hated so.

He took a breath and clamped down on his nerves, decided it was more sensible to go on as he was. He started off, but he didn't get far. Instinct screamed at him, deranging his reason, and within minutes he had stopped again, uncertain and angry. He couldn't ignore the innate urges, like a foreknowledge that gouged him at every step. He broke, finally, mounted and veered off the track to make a wide and probably useless circle, meaning to come back to his own scent trail.

But he didn't make it. Instinct had been right—their scent whispered to him as he crossed the wind barely an hour later. The trace was gone as quickly as it had come, but it had been enough. He was sure of the direction now, if not the exact position. He turned in blessed relief, and in a few moments had caught the scents again, more surely this time—but then he stopped. There was death in this wind, and he shuddered and closed his eyes as the corruption washed over him. But he had smelled death before, and he could control his horror now. He knew this wasn't Cybelle. It was one of the men that was dead.

The horses had caught the scent, too, and the mare snorted, threw up her head. He tightened the rein to keep her from bolting, but she fought him even in her exhaustion. The gelding twitched and sidled nervously away from the battle. Ta Nyahl knew it was as far as he could go this way. Their rebellion would slow him down, give him away if he tried to draw much closer up the wind. He led them off to the side and into a copse of alder, hating to leave them. It made him more vulnerable, and he hardly needed that now. Bitterly he loosened the girths, slipped the bits. He left them scantly tethered, knowing he might never see them again. They were tired now and would wait, but if he didn't return they would pull loose under the pressure of thirst and at least have a chance at life. That thought was hardly a help to his confidence—as if it were a sure premonition he wouldn't be coming back. He started off again, walking now.

Exhaustion stalked him through the night, while he imagined shades of monsters that loomed, only to become a bush or a rock, or a grasping limb. The miasma of death hung in his nostrils like a threat, a tang of unreality that could become himself in one misstep. He limped constantly and staggered sometimes, wondered if the dampness in his boots was blood. His head throbbed. Pain darted through his shoulder at every misstep on the uneven ground. He should have rested, he knew, should have slept. He had been awake too many hours, had pushed his sore body too far, and now he would pay. It was too late. He was in no shape to attempt a rescue—but still he went on. This seemed the only slim chance he had, and stumbling as he was, he wondered why it was so important to him.

Tonight there was no answer for that. There was only walking, and aching, and an automatic gage of the closing distance. He moved more carefully as he neared the camp. A stealth that was innate seized his body, pushing him to the ground, hiding him in the shadows.

It was well past midnight now, and the camp was quiet but not entirely dark. There were fresh logs on the fire, glowing, partially ablaze—a danger to him as it was meant to be. He kept his eyes indirect, found the shapes of the horses, the sleeping form of a man.

His nostrils twitched at the reek. He flinched, wondering how the human could stand to sleep downwind of death that way. But humans were senseless. Perhaps the man couldn't smell the stench at all. He shifted to another vantage in the brush, found a still, slight shape across the firelight. She lay half on her belly, her hands tied around a small tree. Her face looked bruised and swollen, and she lay huddled in a way that made him think she had been hurt. But the fact that she was tied meant she was wasn't badly hurt—she was still dangerous to the man.

It was very hard now for him to do what he must, hard to leave the safety of the brush. The kria were a cautious people, shy and anxious to avoid confrontations of any kind, especially with humans. But the need lay before him, and the sleeping man. Without weapons, without backup— there was only himself to do this, and he had to take his life in his hands. But he would try stealth before an attack. The choice was ingrained, not even something he had to think about.

The night reeled, and he slid out of concealment. He forgot he was lame, forgot he was exhausted. His heart raced, ignited a rush of clarity. Light-headed from exhaustion, breathless, he reached out to touch her wrist.

Her head jerked up immediately, and he snatched his hand away, but as she had in the hollow, she lay still, sounded no alarm. Perhaps she recognized him somehow—or perhaps she thought an animal would be a kinder fate.

He hissed at her faintly—a warning—stole a glance at the man, edged closer. The firelight touched her cheek, the sheen of her hair. Dark and enigmatic, she didn't move. He had his fingers on the cords then, wished with deep bitterness for a knife. It would be only the work of an instant then to free her, or to do this another way—to kill the human, but now he had to work at the knots. The fire shadows licked at him. The human's shape snored raucously by the fire. The woman's hands quivered under his, and her scent drenched him with fear. His heart beat hard, lodged in his throat now, nearly smothering him as he dug in his nails and tugged. The first hitch came free.

The log burst in the fire with a crack, blew angry sparks through the darkness, and the man jerked awake.

He leaped from his blankets already reaching for his weapons. He must have slept with them by his side, through a premonition of danger, perhaps, sensing the hover of death—or because he had captured and harmed a witch. Ta Nyahl had jerked back automatically, ducked into shadows. But it was too late—he had been seen. The man yelled sharply and fiercely, lunged past the fire. A knife flashed like a sliver of flame.

Ta Nyahl galvanized then—he had to. He jerked up to meet the man face to face, and that checked the rush, but it was only for second—long enough for the man to see his prey was unarmed and lighter than himself. Then he slid forward again, his arms spread, the knife held ready before him as he crouched.

It was too many dangers. Ta Nyahl's heart sped, ready to burst. Trapped, aware that Cybelle lay beneath their feet, he forced himself to move cautiously. He gave back—one step—another—hoping to draw the man away into deeper darkness. But the human saw what he meant to do, lunged abruptly to cut him off. He had to dodge sharply away from the knife—dodged again. He saw Cybelle yank at her bonds, heard her curse in a fury.

The man leaped. Ta Nyahl felt a sick dismay then, feeling from his own response that he was too slow. He hadn't any reflexes left. Caught in the man's rush, he slammed against a tree. The impact exploded a sound from him as he lost his breath. The knife blade tore into his skin, seared along his side—but then he had a hand on it.

He wrapped one heel behind the human's, and using the tree for leverage, he arched his spine. The man fell, but he didn't let go of the knife—or of Ta Nyahl. They dropped together, grappled, thrashed. The man was heavier, stronger. He grunted, heaved over on top—a crushing weight that nearly cut off Ta Nyahl's breath.

The horses jerked at their tethers and screamed. Cybelle screamed, too, yelling something he couldn't understand. Ta Nyahl twisted, gasping for breath, grimly fending the knife from his throat. But exhaustion betrayed him then, the weakness of his shoulder. His arm quivered and slipped. The blade fell, but he had known it was coming, writhed aside.

The blade only nicked his ear, sheared hair, and caught in the ground. And in that second instinct took him. The metamorphosis had haunted him through the night and half the day, a degeneration of intellect that pursued him as he tired, and will and repression eroded together. Now it flashed into the firelight, the pure flame of unreason, torn free of any restraints.

It was something the kria didn't do any more—almost unthinkable, buried as it was under the eons of civilization. Prominent as the jaw was, time and atrophy had changed it, shortened the bite. It was inefficient, the fangs blunted by millennia of disuse. But still the potential was there. And this man had no understanding of its implications, no response to the dangers of closeness. He had no idea what he really fought, and he made no move to protect his throat. His weakness drew death to him—the fangs flashed and sank, and the man was dead.

He didn't realize it at first. Ta Nyahl rolled over him and held on. He panted as the man struggled and bled, fended his grasping hands away from the knife—the human might yet kill, if he could get to it. And lying there, he felt a growl rising, a blaze of primitive passions that roared in his ears—the raging bloodlust that had flared with the taste of warm blood in his mouth. It shook him to the core of his being, shrieked in his veins, this killing. Urges assaulted him, obscenities that he could never commit. He knew then why the kria were so constrained to avoid this. The horses' terror hadn't been wrong. They knew what he was.

And Cybelle knew it now, too. She lay quiet as he staggered up finally from the man who was now wholly dead, and caught up the knife. He fell to his knees beside her, cut the cord at her wrist, and she attacked him.

She must have seen the change in his eyes even in the dimness of the firelight. She lunged and struck him across the face, nearly blinding him, and when he had recovered, she was gone.

He lay where he had fallen, shivering at the storm of emotion that raged through him, numb and incapable, and he must have slept—he hardly knew. But as the fire burnt down and the sky began to pale, he woke to the doubled smell of death and knew he had to move.

These men weren't of the band that had followed them the day before. Their clothing, scent and ornaments were those of villagers. The human he had killed lay in a pool of dark blood, his throat mangled and torn, the cartilage and ripped arteries exposed. His dead eyes stared at the sky. In the morning mist, it seemed an act that someone else must have committed, this murder, like something out of a nightmare. The kria were a civilized people. They didn't kill any more with claws and fangs. They didn't lust for blood and butchery. But now Ta Nyahl was covered with the man's clotted blood. He rubbed his hands uncertainly over his face, pushed back his snarled hair, feeling soiled and completely foul, and wondering what was happening to him. It was as if blinders had fallen away suddenly and left him with a different and darker sight. He had proved last night that the hunter was still there within him, and finding it so close left him wondering—could the kria really ever change their nature? Maybe humans were right in their assessment, after all.

But however sickened he felt, he had to move before more humans blundered onto him. He was too close to the village here. And aggravatingly, he still needed to find Cybelle. He must have terrified her with what he'd done, and he regretted it. But he had no right to her horses or her belongings. Regardless that she had run from him, he was sworn to serve her, and even if he was exhausted and disoriented, he still meant to continue that.

He would leave the dead men where they lay, but he wanted their weapons and their supplies. The horses were still terrified of him. He eased up carefully, cajoling them quietly, until he could get at the packs and drag them away to a more comfortable distance.

The other corpse lay there, too, wrapped in a blanket. Even though he hated to get the stench on him, still he peeled back the wrappings to look at it. Cybelle's weapon had left terrible burns charred into the flesh, so deep that the man couldn't have lived for long after she had burnt him. Ta Nyahl resolved to treat the little weapon with proper respect. The man had nothing of value left on him, so Ta Nyahl covered him again with the blanket and went on to search the packs.

He took the food and water skins, found a good quality gray wool cloak that he took for himself—he had rights of conquest, he decided, regardless of the shameful way he had killed the man. The weapons were the best of his prizes. The knives and the arrow points were very fine and one of the bows suited the length of his draw perfectly. He could hardly draw it now, of course, but as his shoulder strengthened it would be more useful. He felt better then, properly outfitted, and hurriedly he repacked the goods, then attacked the project of saddling the horses. He might have to let them go later, but he would rather ride to where he had left Cybelle's animals, if that were possible. It would save his energy and his sore feet. And perhaps she would want to trade. The gelding's continuing lameness made him a chancy mount, whatever his disposition, while these others looked like good horses.

He approached slowly, enduring their trembling and eye-rolling with pained frustration. He needed speed, knowing hostile eyes might chance this way at any time, but he would have to coax them instead, taking care not to frighten them any more. He got the work done as quickly as possible, loaded the packs and with much care, managed to get up on the gentler sorrel. The horse considered bucking, he thought, but he spoke to it and twitched the reins in the human signal it recognized, confusing it. Once they were under way, it settled down to work, given familiar things to do. The other followed unwillingly, pulling back and still rolling its eyes in fright.

He sighed with relief to hear the familiar nicker of Cybelle's obstinate mare as he came close to the thicket where he had left the other horses. The gelding actually came to the end of his tether in greeting, nosed the new supply of feed grain. They were hungry and thirsty, but Ta Nyahl was afraid to stop here, only tugged their tethers loose and turned back to the east as quickly as they would follow. They followed unwillingly, disappointed not to eat, and the mare tried her best to cause trouble, stretching her neck to nip at the strange horses that traveled with them now.

He hadn't enough water in the skins for all of them, and that had to be his first priority. It would be cruel to force them to go any longer without drinking. He knew there was a small spring a few lengths to the southeast that sometimes ran from the thaw this time of the year, and he took the chance, headed that way.

Whether or not he let the captured horses go, he owed them the water, and it would be a reasonable plan to stay there during the day and try to pick up Cybelle's trail in the evening—if the surroundings looked safe enough. He could track her more securely at night when the villagers would be locked inside their palisade, and have the time to rest himself, as well. He was sore and sick and headachy this morning, and his mind was hardly clearer than last night. He needed badly to sleep.

Birds called through the trees, and clear sunlight slanted down through the new green of the leaves. The day was cold after the rain, but the chill wind from the sea had dropped off, and he thought it would be a good day for traveling. He made steady progress, as the horses were fresh and rested. As he went, he kept careful track of the scents and sounds, concerned about running into the large group of men that had been hunting Cybelle. He found no sign of humans, though. The woods only seemed populated by birds and random wildlife today, and he felt easier as he got further away from the village.

The spring was running, as he had hoped. Barely a trickle from the sheared rock of a hill, it collected in a tiny, silt-clogged pool and faded into the ground within a span. He unsaddled the horses and let them drink, then led them back into the brush where they would be well hidden from any prying eyes. Once they were securely tethered, he rolled in the woolen cloak and fell into a sleep like death.

Chapter 9

Ta Nyahl dreamed of his clan. It was a dream he'd often had after his people had died, a recurring nightmare where he had come along the trail and found them all dead. The bodies were scattered among the rough, lean-to shelters. The scent of blood hung over everything, its coppery tang sharp in his nostrils. In the dream state, he walked among the bodies, looking for faces he knew. Here was a child, its throat cut with a knife, there an old woman, her belly sliced open. After a while, he found his mother.

"Mother?" he said.

Her dead eyes looked up at the sky, empty of recognition. She didn't answer. He became aware of his father standing next to him.

"She was my heart," said his father. "What happened to her?"

"She's dead," said Ta Nyahl. "The humans have killed her."

"How did they find us?" asked his father.

"I don't know," said Ta Nyahl.

"Was it sorcery?" asked his father.

Ta Nyahl turned and looked at him. An arrow had pierced his chest, gone through his heart. Blood covered his face from a cut on his brow, ran slowly down his chest and belly. It dripped on the soil at his feet, leaving red pockmarks in the dust.

"I don't know," he said again.

His father looked at him with dead eyes. "What will you do about this, Ta Nyahl?"

"I don't know," he said. "Give me your council."

His father only looked at him, began to fade into nothingness.

The dream broke suddenly as one of the horses stamped and moved in the brush. Ta Nyahl opened his eyes, found the first tinge of morning was lightening the sky. He felt lost and disoriented for a moment, but then he remembered where he was. He had slept all the way through the night. He stirred, took a breath. The dream still felt very real and close.

There was no clue about what it meant.

In the first days after they had found the dead, Ta Nyahl had thought it meant he should take revenge on the humans. It had driven his determination to make the villagers pay, and for a while the raids he and Da Kathan and Da Hanath carried out seemed to help keep the dreams at bay. But now, what he had done had only brought Da Kathan and DaHanath to their deaths.

Lying there, he remembered what Cybelle Lawton had said about a death wish. Looking at things now, he thought probably she was right about his actions. There had been no other possible result for what the three of them had been doing. It was only a matter of time before they were captured and killed. But that thought made him wonder if his interpretation of the dreams had been really correct—or if he had only twisted them for what he wanted. What if his interpretation had only been about his guilt for not being with his clan when they died—about his desire to join them in oblivion? It had taken his near death in the village and Cybelle's intervention to shake him out of that and make him look at living for something else again.

So what was it? What was he supposed to live for? The dream still had an ugly feel—the taste of wrongness. He lay there in his blankets, listening to the sounds of the woods. Closer, one of the horses shifted and switched its tail. It was clear that he needed council, but it was unrealistic to think the dead would provide it, even by way of a dream. They could only speak with their deaths, and through any memories he had of them.

He sighed and tugged his blankets closer around his shoulders in the chill semi-dark. His people felt that dreams had meaning, and that they could provide guidance for what should be done, but the real problem was in interpretation. If he had been in the camp of his clan, he might have consulted a shaman about this one—it had the feel of truth somewhere beneath the images. He tried to put together what he knew now that he hadn't last year, and the conclusion he came to was that all the kria would soon follow after his own clan. It was an ugly thought, but somehow he couldn't escape the cynicism in the way his life had turned during the last year.

After a while the sky grew lighter, and his belly growled. It was a reminder he had forgotten to eat anything the night before. He sat up out of the blankets and ran his fingers through his shaggy hair, tugging out the tangles. He needed to do something about the emptiness inside him soon. The mare whickered, reminding him she was hungry, too.

He got up to attend to the horses first, measured out a portion of grain for each. There was grass in the thicket, too, that they had already feasted on the night before. He lit a small fire then, and started fry bread and onions for breakfast. Around him the scents of the wood were only the native animals. Above in the thicket, a veery thrush warned others away from its territory. In the distance, another one answered.

Ta Nyahl was glad of the respite from humans—he had been in their constant company for days now—but regardless, he couldn't seem to find any internal solace today. He wished he could be done with burdens, and that his life would somehow go back to how it was in the past. He knew it wouldn't happen, though. He was experiencing the effects of choices, and something else, too, he thought—of unlucky chance that had seemed to come upon him from out of nowhere. When other kria seemed to be secure and safe in their lives, he had somehow come to a position where everything was hard and there were no good choices. The world seemed to be changing around him, and all he could see was disharmony and death.

The fry bread and onions were done, and he took the skillet off the fire. The food warmed his belly, made him feel a little better. When he was done, he cleaned the skillet, put it away in the pack. He sat down again, warming by the fire, feeling a temptation to just fade away into the forest. He could live as an outcast the way some other kria did, avoiding anyone and everyone that came from any kind of settlement. He could abandon Cybelle to whatever fate she might find with her own people, never see her again. The idea was attractive in many ways. He felt through it, watching the flames die down to coals in the gathering dawn.

It wouldn't work, he decided. He had obligations and he had to deal with them—his life had no meaning without that.

He scattered the coals, kicked dirt over them to make sure they went out. Then he rolled up his pack and saddled the horses, set off to find Cybelle's trail.

He caught the scents at a turning of the trail that brought him downwind. He had already entered the range of arrow flight, and if he had been human he would have ridden on, out of the last concealment of brush, and probably died. If he hadn't detected the scent he probably would have died anyway—human-outfitted as he was. Before him was only a thin screen of foliage, not enough to stop a powerfully sped shaft. However, the leaves and brush would be an irritation to archers, who would want a clear line of sight. They held their shafts a few seconds yet, and he had a chance to save his life. He caught scent of them, jerked the horses to a stop, and at once threw out his hands to show they were empty.

"Kria-en," he called quickly in his own language. "Do not shoot me."

The mare sidestepped under him in response to his agitation. His heart felt as if it would leap out of his chest. He would have avoided this encounter if he could, and he had no conviction they wouldn't shoot him anyway, once they knew who he was and what he had done.

He held up his hands, away from his weapons, waited for them to look him over, judge the sound of his voice, the way he sat on the horse. The mare shifted her feet again and snorted, uneasy at the scents on the wind, but the pressure of his knees stayed steady, and somehow she behaved.

After a moment, there was a slight sound to his right, and a voice answered him in the kria language.

"Traveler, who are you?"

"I am of Waxing Moon clan," he said. "I am Ta Nyahl."

"Waxing Moon is gone," said the voice.

"It is all I have to claim," he said.

He wasn't sure anymore that he had a right to use the clan name, but it was the only way he had to identify himself in the kria tradition.

"Then where do you go in the human's dress, cousin?"

The question needed a complex answer, but he settled for saying, "I have lost my kria-made clothing. This is all I have to wear just now."

The mare snorted and shifted again.

"May I dismount?" he asked. "The horses will spook if they see you."

"Get down then," said the voice.

Ta Nyahl swung his leg over the pommel and slid out of the saddle. He gathered the horses' reins and held them securely as figures materialized out of the brush. The kria looked to be a hunting party. There were four, lightly armed, and Ta Nyahl dipped his head slightly and spread his hands in the traditional greeting. Their clothing was wool and soft buckskin in forest colors that gave them protective coloration. Humans would never have known they were in the brush. Ta Nyahl had caught their scent, found the faint outlines of their bodies and their weapons because he knew what to look for.

The faces that looked back at him were very similar to his own, the broad, prominent facial bones, the brown skin and the streaked hair of the early spring season. The kria who had spoken to him was the leader of the party. Although the clans lived and traveled separately, they were not so many that Ta Nyahl didn't know his cousins. These were familiar faces, even though he didn't know them well.

"I am Ra Nihn," the kria facing him said. "And these are my brothers Ra Kell and Ra Ahn. We are of the Falling Star clan."

"My father was of Falling Star," said Ta Nyahl. "He was Ta Dahnie who left his clan to live with my mother Na Rahn of Waxing Moon."

"We know Ta Dahnie," said Ra Nihn. "And you. We thought all of Waxing Moon were dead."

"I think I am the last," he said. "I was hunting in the forest when the clan was…slaughtered."

They looked at him in sorrow, knowing what it meant to be without a clan.

"Where are you going Ta Nyahl?" asked Ra Nihn. "You are welcome to rest and take food at our camp."

He considered. It felt important that he find the woman. Still, he felt a bone-deep exhaustion and a need for the comfort of kin. He felt a need to speak with the elders of his people. Cybelle was a complication of their lives that someone else needed to know about—someone better able to deal with the implications than he.

"Thank you," he said. "I will come."

The kria did not have villages. At one time they had built long houses and sheds with palisades as protection in the way humans did, but that had turned out to be too easily attacked and burnt to the ground. Now they kept on the move, traveling from camp to camp in order not to leave too large a footprint that would allow humans to find them.

The Falling Star clan was camped at a spring inside a cane brake that was only a short distance away. The entrance through the cane was a maze that only someone with a sharp sense of smell could have traced. Ra Nihn signaled with a bart bird call as they neared the camp, and Ta Nyahl knew this would warn his kin that the party was bringing home a stranger.

When they broke through on the other side of the cane, the females and children were out of sight and the males were assembled to meet them. He kept his eyes downcast and waited for Ra Nihn to introduce him. He heard a quiet intake of breath from the assembly at the name of his clan. It seemed that all the kria must know that Waxing Moon was gone.

A figure stepped out of the group, a tall kria with many charms braided into his hair. He dipped his head, spread out his hands.

"Welcome to the fire, Ta Nyahl," he said. "I am Ta Marnie, your father's brother. We thought you gone with the rest of the clan. Can you bring us news?"

"I have need to speak with you, uncle," said Ta Nyahl. "But the news I bring is not good."

The introductions continued. Whether or not Ta Nyahl knew these people, it was important to renew the acquaintance through an exchange of names and scents.

Once it was clear that he was indeed kin and safe to have in the camp, the females and children reappeared. The introduction ceremony had interrupted the preparations for the evening meal, and these started up again over campfires between the shelters.

The shelters were temporary, made of cut branches and multipurpose animal skins that could be quickly packed and carried. There were also horses in camp, mostly used as pack animals. Once the introduction of the kin was done, Ta Nyahl unsaddled the four horses, rubbed them down with grass and left them to graze near the spring with the other horses of the camp.

He went then to his uncle's fire. Keeping his eyes respectfully averted, he sat cross-legged across from Ta Marnie where he waited.

"Thassa," he said to Ta Marnie. "I have need of your counsel. I have taken a wrong path, and I am lost."

"Ta Nyahl, I am sorry to hear this," said Ta Marnie.

"There is more," said Ta Nyahl. He had brought Cybelle's black weapon from the saddlebags, and now he unwrapped the cloth to show the thing that lay in his hands.

Ta Marnie didn't offer to touch it. He only looked at it quietly. After a moment he grunted slightly.

"Where did you get this, Ta Nyahl?"

"It belongs to a human woman," he said. "She has..." he groped for a simple way to describe what she wanted, "...has asked me to help her find passage through the mountains."

Ta Marnie thought for another moment.

"You will need to speak to the elders about this," he said. "It is important."

"It is not a good tale," said Ta Nyahl. "I will have much dishonor from it."

His uncle considered that.

"It matters not," he said finally. "We will hear it."

He departed from the fire then to speak with his kin, left Ta Nyahl by the coals. Normally Ta Nyahl would have circulated in the camp, spoken to his cousins, maybe played with the children. But since he was dishonored, he thought he wouldn't be welcome here for very long. He wanted to sit quietly and think about what he needed to say to the council. He felt the eyes of the females of the household on him, but they left him in privacy.

The shadows grew longer, faded into an indigo dusk. After the evening meal, the elders gathered at the center of the camp. There were ten in the council he would speak to, including five males and five females. Ta Nyahl and Ta Marnie arrived early and his uncle sat next to him, offering his support. Ta Nyahl studied the elders as they arrived and took positions by the fire. He was sad and disheartened at the idea of having to describe his failings to this group. They looked stern and uncompromising, and he knew they had little tolerance for those who acted outside the kria traditions. It was something that was seldom done, as it meant one was unsuitable for full participation in the life of the clan. Even small troubles meant that marriage would be difficult to arrange. If the problems were severe enough, then the transgressor was outcast, left to make a life alone. The idea seemed intolerable to the kria, but Ta Nyahl knew he was at that point—no one had to tell him so.

Although he would address the elders, others of the clan had gathered, as well. They sat outside the circle of firelight, ready to listen. When everyone was settled, one of the group spoke. It was Sa Liah, the eldest of the females in the camp. She was still tall and straight, though the blue shadow over her cheekbones had nearly faded into the crevices of wrinkled skin. The amulet braids of her hair sparkled with ornaments.

"Son of Ta Dahnie," she said, "your father's brother has brought you to give us news of the passing of Waxing Moon and events afterward."

"Yes, lhassa," he said. He felt the weight of his transgressions, but he had determined to do this, so he took a deep breath and went on. "This tale does not reflect well upon me, but there may be importance in what I have seen and heard, so I ask that you listen.

"It was in the late fall that Waxing Moon passed," he said, "about the time when the moons cross paths. Those of Waxing Moon clan had seen no sign that there was an attack coming," he said. "The clan was camped to the north of here at the rock bluffs. I rose well before the sun and went out to hunt with my cousins Da Hanath and Da Kathan, as we were in need of stores for the winter. We returned about noon to find that humans were in the camp and that all our people had been slaughtered."

Sa Liah interrupted, "Ta Nyahl, how did they find the camp?" she asked.

"This I don't know," he said, "but I think there may be many things happening that we don't know about. There are strangers in our country."

"Go on, son of Ta Dahnie," said the eldest male, whose name was Ka Tehnie. "Tell us what you did."

"I was angry," he said, "and I led Da Hanath and Da Kathan onto a wrong path. I must take responsibility for this," he said, "as it should not reflect on how they lived their lives. They wanted to follow our ways, to fade away and try to find some place in other clans, but I convinced them that we needed to do something to revenge our people. So we followed the humans back to their village, watched and waited. Through the winter, we harried their people, set fire to their shelters and their stores."

There was a murmur at this, as it was an alternate path that had been discussed in the councils. Still, most were against it.

"This was not a good thing," said Sa Liah. "You may have brought more trouble on us. They will only retaliate."

Ta Nyahl flinched inwardly when she said it. He knew this, and it was one of the things that lay heavy on his heart. But since he had been with Cybelle, he had come to wonder if it really mattered any more.

"Yes, lhassa," he said. "I know that is a danger. I have paid personally for this choice. The humans eventually set a trap for us in the woods. They killed Da Kathan, and captured Da Hanath and myself, took us back to the village for their ritual of torture. Da Hanath died in the village, but I was taken as a slave by a human woman they called a "witch," an ayeen. Her name is Cybelle Lawton. This was several days ago.

"The woman said that the headman owed her for the life of his son, and she asked for me, for Da Hanath's body and for horses and stores in return. We left in the night while the human village slept."

"Where is the woman?" asked another of the females. Her name was Sa Mahn, he remembered.

"I have lost her," he said, "and I am looking for her. I swore I would serve her in order that she would bring Da Hanath's body out of the human village."

There was another murmur at this, but he bore the humiliation. It had been his choice and he had to bear the consequences.

"Elders," he said. "I have one of her belongings that may help explain who she is."

He had laid the cloth-wrapped bundle by his side when he sat, and now he unwrapped it, showed it in the firelight.

"It is a weapon," he said, "that burns the flesh."

They looked at it, the strange materials and the strange workmanship. After a moment Sa Liah held out her hand.

"Give it to me," she said.

Ta Nyahl got to his feet, carried it to her.

"Take care," he said. "It has been used, and dropped."

She took the package carefully, looked at it, touched the dark surface to test its quality. After a moment she passed it to the male who sat next to her. Slowly it traveled around the circle so all could see it. When it had returned to Ta Nyahl, one of the males spoke.

"This is not of our country," he said. "It has come from somewhere else. Ta Nyahl," he said, "what is the woman doing here?"

"Thassa, I do not know," he answered. "She has asked me to help her reach the mountains, and I think she means to go through the pass into the wastelands beyond. However, this has not been an easy task, as a band of human men have pursued us. We stopped at a village so she could trade for supplies, and the humans at the village must have sent word somehow to the men who wanted her. We escaped them, but later she was taken by other men. Elders, I had no weapons, and I have killed one of them with my hands and my fangs."

Another murmur passed at this, but he was almost beyond caring now what they thought. He knew he was lost when Da Kathan and Da Hanath died.

"I have lost her," he said. "And I am bound by the oath. I need to find her."

"We are not so far from The Coming that we have forgotten there are other worlds," said Sa Mahn. "Perhaps the humans know this, too."

"We have seen no sign they know of it," said Ka Tehnie. "Their villages are very primitive."

"There is no sign we know of it," said Sa Liah. "Our camps are more primitive than their villages. Our numbers are failing, and we lose knowledge by the day."

"True words," said Ka Tehnie. "But, Ta Nyahl, do you mean you think there are differences in the humans? Different…nations?"

He considered, and found he was certain of it.

"Yes, thassa," he said. "I think the men pursuing Cybelle Lawton are different from those who live in the villages. They speak differently, and they smell different. They must have a particular reason for wanting her that the villagers do not have."

"So," said Sa Mahn, "either they have the means to make something like this weapon within the wastelands, or it comes from off-world?"

"That is what we must think," said Ka Tehnie.

"There is something else," said Ta Nyahl. It was something that had been nagging at him, something that he had heard while he was waiting for death as a captive of the humans in their village. He closed his eyes, trying to remember what it was that he had overheard. He was very good at the human's language. Not realizing it, they had spoken of many things that he had caught and at least partially understood. He had been weakened by blood loss and pain, sliding in and out of consciousness, but now he searched, trying to put together the remnant of memories.

"The villagers spoke of a 'bounty,'" he said. "This was a word I had heard used in this way before. I think it means that there is a payment for evidence of every kria that is killed."

They looked at him, as if dumfounded. It was not a concept that the kria could easily understand.

"You mean that someone is paying for every kria that is killed?" asked one of the males, Ka Nahnie. "Paying what?"

"I don't know," said Ta Nyahl. "Perhaps supplies, horses, weapons—these thing would be a price, wouldn't they?" He went on. "What I mean is that someone among the humans has determined that the kria should all die—all the clans, in the way that Waxing Moon died."

There was silence for several moments while they absorbed this.

"In that case, will it matter what path we take?" asked Sa Mahn, looking around the circle.

It was what had concerned Ta Nyahl earlier. These things meant it didn't matter what the council decided. It didn't matter how careful and circumspect they were in trying to live in the same land with the humans, or whether they tried to move elsewhere, or whether they tried to fight back against the aggression. If someone was paying for them all to die, then it made little difference what they did.

"Ah," said Sa Liah. "This is much to think on. The all-clan council will need to know."

The others in the council stared at her.

"Ta Nyahl," she said. "Is there anything else?"

"No," he said. "Except that I am in a situation I don't understand. Will you take the weapon?"

"We have seen it," she said. "It is not ours to take. Give it back to the woman if you can find her."

She addressed the circle. "Is there anything else? If not, we are done here."

There seemed to be nothing else. She rose sharply, strode away into the darkness. Some of the others glanced at Ta Nyahl as they got up from the cross-legged positions of the circle. He thought there was concern in their eyes. He sat with his head down, wondering at the resolution of this meeting. After a moment, his uncle's hand rested on his shoulder.

"Are you all right, nephew?" he asked.

"Yes," he said. "What am I to think, uncle?"

"They have not condemned you," said Ta Marnie. "Nor have they welcomed you to stay." He stopped, took a breath. "The news you bring is disturbing. Sa Liah wishes not to have heard it."

"I should go, then," he said.

"Stay the night at my fire," said Ta Marnie. "It won't hurt you to rest with us a while."

Ta Nyahl rewrapped the black weapon in its cloth and got to his feet. Once he was standing, he saw that Ka Tehnie was waiting at the edge of the firelight. The old kria meant to speak to him.

"Elder," he said, lowering his eyes.

Ka Tehnie moved into the firelight. He reached out and put his hand on Ta Nyahl's shoulder.

"Ta Nyahl," he said, "this is sad news you bring us."

"Would that I hadn't," said Ta Nyahl.

"Would we rather not hear of our own deaths?" asked Ka Tehnie. "It is better that we know, I think. This way we can make some kind of preparation."

Ta Nyahl took a breath.

"What's to become of me, thassa?" he asked faintly.

"Nothing happens without cause," Ka Tehnie said. "Go with the woman, Ta Nyahl, and find your own way. We are fewer than we were in my youth—we are dying here, only a remnant of what we are supposed to be. The humans may be killing us for the bounty, as you say, but we can't change any more and remain what we are. Even this disagreement with our traditions is too much for us to deal with easily. But your position isn't all bad, my son. You are young and free of us, free to find a new way, unencumbered by the old, and you must do what you can for the future."

It seemed to be a release and a blessing both. He felt it descend on him as he lay in his uncle's shelter that night, waiting for sleep to come.

Chapter 10

The morning dawned pale and misty, shot through with gold. Inside the canebrake, spiders had woven webs overnight that captured the dew. The canes arched overhead, casting a pattern against the light. A veery thrush announced the sunrise, but the camp was already stirring.

Ta Nyahl didn't mean to linger. He rose with the sun and broke fast with his kin, set to work immediately in making up his packs to leave. His uncle's household had supplies ready to send along with him. He left the extra horses as a gift for his kin, saddled Cybelle's mare and the bay and lashed the packs behind the saddles.

When he was done with that, he returned to his uncle's fire. He found that Ka Tehnie was sitting there, too. Ta Nyahl spread his hands and dipped his head in greeting.

"Elder," he said, "may the day treat you well."

"Sit with us," said Ta Marnie. "Ka Tehnie has come to speak with you."

It was a surprise. Ta Nyahl sat with them before the fire, kept his eyes respectfully downcast.

"Young one," said Ka Tehnie, "I have brought you something."

He lifted a small bundle from beside him. It was an ivory hair pin that he unwrapped from the folded doeskin, smooth and yellowed with age. The long shaft was carved with symbols and script, charms to preserve the soul of the wearer.

"I had this from my father," said Ka Tehnie. He leaned and presented it with both hands, a gesture that showed its importance. "May it bring you blessing," he said, "and ward away evil."

The pin was meant to fasten a warrior's braid. It was a treasure with meaning that couldn't be replaced. As an outcast, Ta Nyahl shouldn't be given this kind of gift—but he couldn't refuse it. He stretched out both hands to take it.

"I am unworthy," he said, "but I welcome your blessings, thassa. Thank you."

When Ka Tehnie had chanted the blessing that went with the gift and gone, he sat there, fingering the fine texture and carving of the ornament, wondering at the sentiment that brought it to him. His uncle's wife Sa Rahn came up beside him, reached down to touch his shoulder.

"Ta Nyahl," she said. "I will braid up your hair for you."

He looked up at her in surprise. "But I'm not a warrior," he said.

"You don't need the rite," she said. "If you are all that's left of your clan, then you are their last warrior. Ka Tehnie knows this. He brought you the pin for a reason."

She braided his hair for him, twisted it into a warrior's knot at the back, as if he were going off to war, and secured it with the ivory pin. When he reached up to touch it, Sa Rahn laid her hand on his.

"Child, it comes with responsibility," she said, "regardless of whether you have completed the ceremony."

That was something he hadn't thought about, and the responsibility added an extra burden to his shoulders. The pin didn't really mean that anything had changed in his life. He was still an outcast, still the slave of a human woman. But it did mean that Ka Tehnie had given him a kind of direction for his future.

"Thank you," he said to her.

"Our prayers will follow you," she said. She touched his shoulder again, left him at the fire with Ta Marnie to go about her morning chores.

Ta Nyahl hadn't forgotten what it was the human woman wanted from him. Before he left, he needed information on the mountains.

"Uncle," he said. "Will you tell me about the route through the mountains?"

Ta Marnie laid aside the arrow he had been fletching.

"It's been many years since I've been to the peaks," he said, "but I will tell you what I know. The trail you've been following up the mountain leads to the best pass, but there is also another way through the crags. It's a little further south. It's a harder path, but if you are being followed, you shouldn't take the obvious route."

"How will I find it, uncle?" he asked.

"Look for the rocks to make the shape of a ram," said Ta Marnie. "Then keep the formation over your right shoulder as you climb."

He bowed his head. "Thank you, uncle," he said. "I will do as you say."

There was more information on what to expect. He listened carefully, committing the details to memory. As he started to take his leave, his cousin Ra Nihn came to tell him the woman was headed southwest, and wasn't that far away.

She came up the rise without detecting him, raised her head to find him there before her, silently waiting. She caught her breath, jerked to a stop, and stood poised like a deer surprised by a hunter. Her eyes were dark and wild.

He thought she would run from him again, and he dropped to one knee and ducked his head in submission. Still he could tell her impulse was to run.

"Lhassa," he tried, desperate to be rid of the burdens that lay on him, "please."

She stopped. "What do you want?" she asked in a shaky voice.

"Take your things—the horses." He thrust the reins out at her, wishing to be free of that guilt, at least—that he rode horses that were hers while she struggled through the woodlands afoot, in boots that must hurt like his had when he had walked too far in them.

The mare snorted at his abruptness, and Cybelle trembled visibly. The fringe quivered on her jacket, dancing at the edge of his vision. The two of them seemed balanced for an instant on the point of a knife, ready to fall in any direction. He waited, frozen, for her decision. When she gave no indication of it, he risked a glance upward.

There was only horror in her face.

He let go of the reins, pushed upward then and swung about sharply, meaning to take himself away from her. It was the only rational thing to do, if they could find no understanding. He wouldn't impose his presence on her—and he couldn't bear to be so near her disgust. He took three steps through the sodden leaves.

"Wait," she said.

Her voice was sharp and uneven, near to breaking. He stopped, trembling himself now with the strain, with the rebuff, with the memory of what stood in her eyes.

"Ta Nyahl..." she said. Then after a moment he heard her draw a breath. "Why are you doing this?" she asked.

"They are yours, lhassa," he said, without looking around. "Not mine."

"That's not what I meant," she said.

Failing to understand that, he only continued to wait.

"I mean..." she said, and then stopped again. "You could go. Do you really mean to come back to me?" she asked. Her voice trembled. "Regardless?"

"It is all I have left, lhassa," he said simply.

"All you have left? I don't understand that. How can I trust you?" she asked.

He flinched inwardly, but he kept his voice even, and gave her no indication it. She was judging him in human terms after all, of which he had some understanding.

"If you cannot," he said, "then I will go."

Silence lay between them for a matter of moments.

"Alright. Don't go," she said. She sat down abruptly.

He turned. The horror was gone from her eyes, but what they held now was hardly less comfortable, and her face was very white. His own gaze slid away, came to rest on the horses, a place that held no pain—regardless that the mare still hated him viciously. At least it was mindless hate.

"Do you have something to eat?" asked Cybelle.

He got cheese and bread out of the saddlebags and gave them to her, waited, sitting silently with his eyes downcast, for her to eat. But now that he knew she would go with him, he was fretting internally. If the kria knew where she was traveling, then others would, as well.

"We shouldn't stay here on the trail," he said finally. "Will you ride now, lhassa?"

She ducked her head and rubbed at her face tiredly, rose and stepped toward the horses, but then she shied as he moved to help her. He stood back for her to mount, holding the gelding and keeping a clear distance away from her. He handed her up the reins, still without touching. Then he got up on the mare himself.

"Will you still go to the mountains, lhassa?" he asked.

"Yes," she answered faintly.

He took his bearings, and set off to the southwest.

It was late afternoon, and Ta Nyahl thought there would soon be barely light enough left in the day to find a safe campsite. Rest had done the gelding good, and his limp seemed nearly gone, so they would be able to make good time. But still it wouldn't be wise to press the horse in a chase.

No more words passed between him and Cybelle. She rode in silence, and he wondered, again what it was that drove her, what quest had put her into this forest alone, alien as she was. It hinted at events he didn't know of, and that he thought now that he should know about. It had been growing on him that it was important. His kind had accepted the humans here as they'd found them, but now he knew they were something more, as well—as the kria had been—and that their affairs stretched wider by far than anyone here had known.

As if by magic, sloughing old angers had changed his perceptions, and new ones were settling around him—of what the kria were, and what place they had in this world, and in the wide darkness outside of it. Suddenly the clans that he had always thought as solid as the world were only fragile constructions of tenuous souls, and he feared for them. What they had was little force to keep a wide eternity at bay, that was so fraught with perils and unknowns.

He wanted to ask if Cybelle still thought pursuit was close behind her. He wanted to ask why the men wanted her, and who they were. The questions ached in him like fire, but he smothered them down without even glancing back at her. Her silence and the whiteness of her face as he had last seen it disinclined him. And he thought it hardly mattered. His duty was to her. Or would it be, he thought with a shiver, if he knew the whole situation? Because now he was sure something was going on beyond his knowledge that might reshape this world. And he had been born here, after all. His people were out there, living in it as best they could.

Ta Nyahl found a likely campsite on the edge of dusk. It was a thick copse of alder and evergreen grown round with vines, with a trickle of water nearby. He reined in the mare.

"This is a good place for the night," he said. "Will you camp here, lhassa?"

"Yes," she said, again faintly, in a voice that seemed unlike her own. It worried him.

He dismounted and forced his way into the matted fortress, hacking out a narrow, unobtrusive passage. He found, as he'd expected, that shade made vegetation sparse within the palisade of trees. Here, he would even risk a fire.

He set about unsaddling the horses and unloading the packs, and finally went to find solid wood for the night's fire. All this time Cybelle sat on a fallen log—as if dazed, he thought, and he became more worried at her look of emptiness. But as darkness fell and the lick of flame rose up the first logs, she seemed to grow more alive. She moved toward its comfort, and he thought she must be only tired. He got out supplies and to make bread as she had before to go with stew, thinking she must still be hungry. Foraging in the woods was tiresome, and tended to delay traveling, or else to delay eating. And if she wasn't hungry, he was. He thought she shivered as the dew fell.

The bruises on her face were very dark, and one of her eyes was swollen. Her wrists were marked, too, from ropes that had been too tight.

"Are you cold?" he asked, his hands busy.

She looked up from the flames, as if startled. "I..." she began, and then stopped. "Yes," she said quietly. "I guess. A little."

He tugged a blanket out of the pack and stepped over, draped it around her shoulders, went back to shaping the bread.

"Is your hair changing color?" she asked.

He glanced up.

"Yes," he said, and realized then how little she knew of the kria. Of course she might be a foreign woman, but at that, still she might know more than the humans born here. His hair was turning a warm, dark brown. "With the spring," he added.

She propped her elbows on her knees, seemed to consider that with more energy than she had shown yet today. "It changes with the season?" she asked. "White in the winter? Brown in the summer?"

"Yes," he admitted, uncertain why she wanted to know this. It left him vaguely uncomfortable. It was even worse when she laughed suddenly, and gave no explanation for it. He squirmed slightly, but he wouldn't ask why she laughed. He only left her to privacy. He had enough dark thoughts of his own to occupy him, after all, without delving into hers. And he still had his pride.

"You're a carnivore," she said then.

He blinked this time, surprised that she said it so openly—the thing that must have so horrified her before—but he didn't look up at her. It felt like an attack, and as much as he wanted to face it, he wouldn't. Hostility between them wouldn't be of any help.

"Yes," he managed, evenly enough, though his face grew hot.

"It's why the horses are afraid of you."

"Yes," he admitted again. He sat still, watching the bread on the fire, holding his hands still, carefully trapped between his knees.

"You're very well controlled, so much that…I hadn't realized it," she said. "What does it mean for you to look straight at me?" she asked. "A challenge?"

He hesitated, still feeling pressed, but determined to get along with her. Humans had never tried to understand the kria, and somehow he found her questions threatened him, as if they could be a danger.

"Yes," he said. "Aggression. Sometimes other things."

"Well, damn, I guess I have the key to the facial expressions now," she said bitterly. She lifted her hands abruptly to rub at her face. "I'm sorry," she said then. She rocked back and forth, as if in pain, dropped her hands. "Maybe I shouldn't ask these things."

"It doesn't matter," he said simply. And he found it didn't.

The bread was done. He bent over the fire, lifted it into a bowl and served the thickened stew to place beside it.

"Will you eat, lhassa?" he asked, and offered it to her.

She took it and wolfed down the food, as he ate his own more sparingly. She must have been ravenous.

He thought she must be exhausted, so he stood the first watch, and she slept the way she had eaten, ravenously, as if she hadn't slept for days. There was a massive tree to one side of their campsite, and he sat at the base of it, hidden in the comfortable shadow. The night wore on, the stars turning above him, making familiar patterns. The sounds and scents formed familiar shapes around him, as well. Bridets and cicadas sang from close by. A don'will called from somewhere distant, plaintively seeking for a mate. Even further away, he caught the faint roar of a las bear and the shrill yips of baywolves from higher on the mountains.

The largest moon rose, and the blue one close behind. Their light cast complex and shifting shadows in the woods, making apparitions like dreams that he knew weren't real. It was as if his thoughts took shape, and he saw people in his mind's eye that were gone now. He could think over conversations he had held with Da Hanath, or with his father or brother, and they lived for a while in his memory. He could imagine conversations he might be having now, but he knew that was really rising from inside himself. He wondered if the visions were useful, or trustworthy in any way. He sighed and shifted his seat, keeping stiffness away.

The wind eddied, bringing the scent of the forest behind him, the faint trace of a fox, attracted by the smell of their cooking. High up in the tree, a bart bird stirred and twittered, perhaps disturbed by a dream.

Cybelle screamed suddenly.

Ta Nyahl started, jerked up and around desperately, thinking he had dozed and missed some attack. But there was nothing that should have frightened her—only the usual scents and the noises of the night.

She was standing on her feet, the blankets fallen too near the fire. He snatched them away, and as he moved toward her, she shied backward. He stopped.

"Lhassa?" he said, uncertainly.

She was trembling visibly and her eyes were wide and wild. He thought she would run into the woods again, and he stepped forward quickly to catch her. She struggled so he had to tighten his arms to hold her, and he realized she wasn't really awake. She must have had a nightmare.

"Lhassa!" he said, holding her, and it apparently penetrated whatever dream she labored within. She lay stiffly against him a moment; and then suddenly the strength went out of her and she almost fell, just as he had begun to let go of her. He had to catch her quickly.

"What was it?" he asked.

"I…" she said. And then, "Nothing, I guess. A dream."

She was trembling against him now, though standing with her own strength again. He started to let go of her and move away, but she held on to him fiercely.

"No," she said. "No. Just a moment."

Her voice sounded strange, and as he stood, she let her head fall on his shoulder. When her shoulders heaved with a convulsive shudder, he realized she was weeping. It was something humans did when they were upset, and then he understood that she wanted him there for comfort. It was a strange role, and awkward, but not that bad, so he continued to wait while she stood there and cried on his shoulder.

After a time the sobbing movement of her shoulders ceased and she was quiet. He wondered if he should let go of her then, but she continued to hold onto him. She moved finally, lifted her head and pressed her lips against his throat.

He started back at that, thinking she meant to bite, and she laughed suddenly, tearfully, and wiped her eyes.

"I'm sorry," she said, and sniffed, but she held to him even more tightly then, so it would be awkward if he tried to move away from her. And he wasn't really afraid of her in that way. He stayed where he was.

"What was that?" he asked, after a moment of wondering.

"A kiss," she explained. "It's a gesture of affection."

"Oh," he said, and found it wasn't so obscure after all.

The noises of the woods settled around them again, resuming the songs that had been disturbed by her outcry.

The interrupted cries of bridets and cicadas started up, then the don'will, and somewhere a veery thrush warned others away from its place in the darkness.

And Ta Nyahl found himself suddenly wondering if humans and kria were sexually compatible. He found that, like her scent, Cybelle's warmth and the curves of her body weren't unpleasant against him, and he stifled an incipient urge to nuzzle her ear, closed his eyes against the desire.

Human men raped kria females without doing excessive damage. At first it had seemed a strange thing to the kria, among whom rape was a bizarre aberration, and it had quickly become a matter for contempt, that human men would take anything they could beat into submission. But now he wondered if they didn't understand a fundamental similarity between the races that somehow the kria hadn't seen.

The possibility of his desire for her spoke of other things, as well—if that was what this was. His estrangement from the kria had loomed large in the last weeks, and he had found that once his hatred for humans was broken, he had fallen into a confusion that made him question all he had learned in his life, even to the fundamental values. And now he was falling prey to instinct and emotion, without regard to sense.

If he wanted this woman, would it be so wrong to take her? He was stronger, and probably he could do it without difficulty, as a human man would.

At the thought he felt the need for her expand suddenly within him, and it shook him like an earthquake—not only the desire, but the warring of mores with intent. He caught his breath, and felt a painful, violent trembling begin somewhere, deep inside of him.

Cybelle dropped her arms and stepped away.

It startled him and he let go of her as well. But she seemed not to have felt the change in him, the shudder of desire. She sniffled loudly and wiped her eyes again, looked for something in her pocket to blow her nose on.

"I'll stand watch now," she said. "I'm certainly awake. And, you know, I haven't said 'thank you,' Ta Nyahl. I should have, more than once in the past few days."

It was like cold water on his skin, though he hardly heard what she said to him. His heart was pounding, and his muscles shook like branches in a storm. He closed his eyes, took a sharp breath.

"I don't think I can sleep, lhassa," he said, "for a while." There was a tremor evident in his voice, and she looked at him oddly.

"I only had a bad dream," she said. "What is it? Is something wrong?"

"Nothing," he said, letting out his breath carefully. "I will lie down anyway, lhassa."

It sounded stiff and it was. He lay in his blankets, feeling wounded, and wondering whatever had come over him. He felt angry and hurt at her insensitivity, but after an uncomfortable while his shaking fell off to mere discomfort, and he found he could consider his responses more rationally.

She had wanted comfort, and he had reacted appropriately enough to that. It was no more than she had tried to give him before, he thought, and he had almost learned the elements of what she expected when he had been hurt and frightened himself. But then something else had happened, and he couldn't blame her if she hadn't sensed it. Human women weren't the same as kria women, after all.

Cybelle's shadow moved in his perception, and he opened his eyes to a slit, but she was only tending the fire. She laid a log on the flames and then drifted away from the firelight, where her dark shape leaned against a tree again and pulled the blanket tight around her shoulders.

He continued to watch her silently, lying wound in his own cocoon of blankets. Finally he realized there was an intrinsic change in the relations between them for him to have thought of her as he had. It was to do with how he considered himself, and her, and he realized then why she had so little trust in him, and in his intentions. Perhaps she saw more clearly than he. In the past weeks, he had altered from a civilized kria to an animal and back again. He had become outcast from his own people and had been forced into acceptance of his enemy as a real people. Somehow all that had opened the gaping chasm at his feet that he had nearly fallen into just now, on the point of forgetting his oath to Cybelle—and also the reasons for which the kria gave respect.

He sighed and shifted irritably. If he was never again to be allowed among the kria, should their tenets still bind him? Should they still have meaning in his life? Perhaps instead he should make up his own rules now as he went along. The thought was cynical, but after a moment's reflection, he realized that it was cold and sober truth, to an extent, and frightening. He would have to find his way in the world now with no elders to guide him, and he would certainly encounter problems and urges that other kria didn't have to deal with.

He sighed and rearranged the blankets again, unable to find any comfort in these thoughts. Already he had done things that would otherwise have been unthinkable, and it might be that he should adopt human ways, or human expectations, and become a predator—with Cybelle as his first victim—in order to protect himself. But he thought that would destroy him.

And of course, it would. He could see the wisdom of his elders clearly of a sudden, the reasons they kept the young so close, and so carefully guarded the clans. For that was what made the kria, and gave them an identity by which to live their lives, under whatever circumstances. Near proximity to the humans and their startling ways had made no change in that. He, himself, was now just on the verges of control, clanless, motherless, and by slipping outside he had doomed himself. There was a reason that the kria had no place for him any longer.

He had been loved and respected, though. In his bitterness he hadn't realized how important that was until it was gone. That had not kept the kria from sending him away, as he had thought it wouldn't. He had become a danger to the community by his necessity to follow other ways. When he had first felt his estrangement, he hadn't understood the reasons for it. But now that he had seen the chasm of nothingness that lay before him, and knew what he could become, he realized the reasons for their rules and their insistence on following tradition. He thought then that he loved those among the kria in return who still loved him. However, that meant they imprisoned him, and that it was too late for him to change what he was. That thought blasted him to nothingness—and then he felt his life solidify again. As if he had reaffirmed everything that made him what he was, he embraced the whole set of beliefs and values and behavior patterns. He would be kria through and through until he died, regardless.

He lay there for a while longer listening to the pulse that still hammered in his ears, feeling the heat that lay in him, and then he sat up. The last moon had risen, and its light penetrated through the thicket in a silvery reflection of daylight, almost dimming the embers of fire. Alert and uncertain, standing against the massive tree, Cybelle glanced toward him as he moved.

"Are you still awake?" she asked quietly.

He didn't answer, but pushed the blankets aside and rose to his feet. This was a risk, and not a risk, he thought, having made up his mind what he was—at least for the time being. He crossed the glow of the firelight and stopped in front of her. As she looked at him inquiringly, he leaned across and set one hand on either side of her, trapping her against the tree. Then he leaned and touched his nose to her ear.

Besides the sensual quality of his warm breath, it was a gesture that offered his throat to her without reservation. It wouldn't have come as a surprise to a kria woman, as there would have been a period of courtship preceding it and the surety of scent. He thought that Cybelle wouldn't recognize the gesture, anyway. But still he did it—for his own pride—and for the possibility that he might still sleep a few hours tonight.

He felt the quiver of her fear begin. She was caught, unsuspecting, against the tree with him in a dominant and threatening position. She quickly put her hands against his chest to push him away, but he stayed where he was, close to her with his hands against the tree on either side of her. He wasn't touching her really—only waiting. She froze very still, as if waiting, too, and he thought suddenly and awkwardly that he would have to explain what this meant. But his closeness and warmth and the heat of his breath must have been clear enough.

"Does this mean what I think it does?" she asked finally, in an unsteady voice.

He drew back slightly so he could see her face, feeling for an answer, and finding none that would serve.

"If I say 'no,'" she asked, in a voice that trembled frankly, "what will you do then?"

The look in her eyes was terror. He sat back on his heels, giving her space, and took a breath, thinking that he had his answer now, clear enough.

"Nothing," he said. "I only wanted you to know."

He went back to his blankets then, and slept until the sun rose.

Chapter 11

It was chilly in the pale light of morning, so much so that he almost expected frost in his hair. He remained in the cloak of his blankets for a while after he wakened, loath to give up the warmth and comfort. He had grown spoiled with just one night in the kria village, however humiliating the stay had been in other ways. Now he hated to get up and face the hardships of the day.

He felt very comfortable lying there. His physical wounds were nearly healed, with only a lingering stiffness and pain in his hurt shoulder. Perhaps some of his psychic wounds were healing, too, he thought, the heavy burden he had carried from the loss of his kin. He felt freer and easy somehow, filled with wellbeing. If he had been alone he would have slept a while longer, until the sun was warm. But he thought Cybelle might have a different opinion of the matter, harried and delayed as she already was. Finally he stirred and sat up in the pale pre-dawn.

She turned her head as he moved, still a dark shape sitting against the gray-barked tree. Her eyes flicked away, uncertain, and one of her hands slid out of the blankets to wipe her hair back from her face, slid back inside again. He thought she looked tired and almost wan, though it could have been the light.

He hugged his arms around his ribs, feeling the chill penetrate where the blankets had fallen away.

"We should be climbing the mountain today," he said in a voice that was husky from the damp.

When she nodded faintly, he rubbed his hands over his face and pushed back the ragged strands of his hair. He got up and carried his blankets to her, and she watched him approach with an obvious disquiet. She pulled her feet up as he got close, but he ignored that, and spread the still-warm blankets into a pallet on the ground before her.

"Sleep for a while," he offered. "I'll bring wood and water and make breakfast."

She stared at him and nodded, rolled onto the blankets quietly.

He brought the wood first and built up the fire, and then fed the horses. As they ate he tugged the ivory pin that Ka Tehnie had given him out of his hair, combed the strands smooth. Then he braided and twisted them up tightly again into the warrior's knot at the nape of his neck, caught the twist firmly with the pin. It was a little difficult with the sore shoulder, but it was such a relief to control the wild mass that he bore the pain gratefully. He fingered the fine-carved shaft. It was abrim with memories that he thought he would treasure always. Regardless if something should happen to the ornament, the gift was permanent and it would endure within him. He brushed the uneven hair in front out of his eyes, regretting its raggedness and the loss of his amulet braids, but the ragged wisps of bangs weren't even long enough to tuck behind his ears. He would have to bear with them in his eyes a while longer.

Warmer now from the activity and the fire, he brought the water and finished bread for breakfast, cutting cheese to go with it this time, and took Cybelle a cup of tea. She stirred at the sound of his boots coming closer, as if she had only been dozing.

Her eyes flickered away from him again, and he realized then what she was thinking, felt his face grow hot. He bent to one knee and offered the cup.

"I'm sorry," he said. It seemed necessary to apologize.

She looked up sharply. "I...no. I...don't know..." she said, which generally mystified him. But she took the cup and looked at him more directly, as was her habit—which perhaps indicated it had been right to apologize, after all. He had to feel his way with her.

"Are you hungry?" he asked, and she nodded, followed him back to the fire, trailing the blankets behind her like a child, and settled again.

They began to eat in silence, but after a moment she was watching him again, not steadily, only glancing at his face now and then as if studying the lines of it. He refused to let it bother him, and only stared at the horses idly. Rays of the sun cut through the trees suddenly, illuminating the glade.

"What happened to the front of your hair?" Cybelle asked.

He started slightly, realized she had been watching him comb and twist it up as he thought she slept. Probably she could see from the unevenness and his irritation with it how it had been sawn off so roughly.

"It was cut off," he said.

"I could see that," she said.

After a moment, when he didn't say anything more, she said faintly, "I was only trying to make conversation. If you don't want to tell me…"

"There were amulets braided into it," he said, still planning to get along with her today, whatever it took. "Good wishes."

"Good wishes?"

"From my kin," he said.

"What happened to them?"

"They're dead," he said. It sounded too harsh.

"I'm sorry," she said. And he thought her face flushed hotly, but she turned away so he couldn't see. "I only meant to ask about the charms," she explained after a moment. "I didn't mean to offend you."

"They were ornaments," he said, "of different workmanship that I received as gifts when I was a child, silver and moonstone, some of them, or copper."

"Oh," she said again, as if realizing what had happened. "Then I guess I know how you lost them."

"Yes," he agreed, relieved that he wouldn't have to review the whole story now. She knew the end of it anyway.

But thinking back on those things reminded him of something he had entirely forgotten, something that he had of hers.

"Wait," he said. "I have something for you."

He finished the last of his tea, gulped it down to empty the cup, and then rose to search through the saddlebags for the package he had for her, wrapped in oiled cloth.

She looked at it in his hands, mystified, and then put down her bowl to take it from him and unwrap it slowly. Seeing what it was, she glanced at him sharply. But he had been ready for some reaction, and kept his face expressionless. He only sat down again and watched for what she would do with it.

"Where did you get this?" she asked.

"I found it near the berry thicket," he admitted, evenly but with some remorse for having forgotten it.

She touched one of the levers, changing the setting, which likely made it safer to carry, he thought.

"Do you know what it is?" she asked.

"I know, lhassa." He didn't think it would be wise to completely deny it, since he knew exactly. She would be able to read that in his eyes.

"How?"

"I...saw the man you killed with it."

"Oh," she said. She reached one hand out suddenly, as if to touch his chin, but stopped this time before she completed the gesture. He recognized it well enough though, and knowing what she wanted, he raised his eyes evenly to her face, met hers.

"You've never seen another one?" She had caught the flicker of his interest as she adjusted it, but he was ready for this, too.

"No, lhassa," he said. "Nothing like that."

It was the truth, and he could believe it, but of course it wasn't all the truth. She accepted it, but she searched his face, and still looked suspicious when she was done.

"I wish you hadn't seen it," she said.

That had meaning, and he sat for a moment thinking about what it was. The kria elders had agreed that it was a foreign-made weapon, and that surely meant she was foreign to this country, as well. If the kria elders were correct that the technology was from off-world, then it likely meant that Cybelle was from off-world, too. This he already knew. But her reasons for being here were still unknown to him, as was the cause for the pursuit and the attempts by other humans to capture her.

He picked up a small stick from the earth before the fire, rolled it between his fingers. He was having second thoughts now about his own silence, his unwillingness to give her information about the kria. He hated to disrupt the fragile understanding they seemed to have this morning, but perhaps it was time to ask her about these things.

"Lhassa," he said, "where does the weapon come from?"

She looked over at him sharply at that, but he kept his eyes on the twig rolling between his fingers.

"It's not something you need to know," she said.

He considered that. She had hidden the weapon from him before and now refused to discuss it. The human villagers had called her a witch, apparently without any idea that she might have come from somewhere else. The conclusion was that she didn't want anyone to know that she was here or what she was doing. But now he felt a burden to understand what was going on.

"Lhassa," he said. "I do need to know."

There was no answer, and after a moment he glanced over. She was staring at him with a serious expression. She didn't seem angry, but there was no clue to what she was thinking. He wouldn't give up.

"Lhassa," he said, "will you listen if I tell you about the kria?"

She moved suddenly, wrapped the black weapon in the cloth again and laid it aside.

"That is something I need to know about, myself," she said. "Go ahead and tell me."

"During the time we were separated, I have been to the camp of my people," he said.

"How did it go?" she asked. Likely she was remembering what he had said about not being able to go back.

"It wasn't what I expected," he admitted. "I have taken many wrong paths, and I expected punishment. But I brought many questions, too, that will have to be dealt with."

He glanced at her, but she was only waiting.

"The kria have a tradition about The Coming," he said. "They came to this world from the sky, where they had suffered hardship. They made a home in the forest far to the south of here, near the sea. They established clans and went about their lives. However, as they ranged northward, they encountered humans, first hunters, and then larger bands of warriors. At first the two people got along fairly well, trading in ideas and goods, but later relations began to go bad as more of the kria came northward to escape storms from the sea.

"The kria are very careful, very respectful and very rooted in tradition," he said. He felt it was important to tell her this, as he thought she might not understand it. "They do not… make war in the way the humans do. As relations failed with the humans, they tried to withdraw. However, this didn't seem to help. There was much discussion about what to do, and the clans gave up building villages, went to camps instead that could be easily moved.

"I am of Waxing Moon clan. In the fall," he went on, "Da Hanath, Da Kathan and I went out before the sun rose to hunt, and when we returned, there were humans in the camp, and the people of Waxing Moon clan were all dead." This was the part he had told the elders at the kria camp, but now it seemed to hold less shame for him, and he said it easily enough. "I wanted to act in revenge instead of acceptance, and I convinced my cousins that we should fight back and make the humans pay for slaughtering our kin. You saw the result. We did it successfully for a while, but eventually Da Kathan was killed in the woods, and Da Hanath and I were captured."

He had thought she might be angry that he had wanted revenge against her people, but like the kria elders, she only listened quietly. Now that he had stopped, though, she had questions.

"It was the Tanner village that sent warriors to kill your kin? You're sure?" she asked.

He had to think a moment about what she meant, but then he remembered the headman in the village was called Tanner.

"Yes," he said. "The three of us followed them back to their village. And something else," he went on. "As I waited to die in the human's village, I heard them say there would be a bounty for my death, and that of Da Hanath."

"A bounty?" she asked.

Her question didn't seem to need a reply. From her voice, she must know what the word meant even better than he. It gave him more confidence that he had understood it correctly.

"What do you mean that the kria 'came to this world from the sky'?" she asked, after a while. "Do you know?"

He gathered his determination to talk about this, and told her what the elders said it meant.

"The kria are not native here. They came from another place, off-world," he said.

"Ah," she said.

Ta Nyahl was growing surer that this woman was from off-world, as well. She wasn't surprised at the idea at all.

"How long ago?" she asked. "How many years?"

"In human years, I don't know, lhassa," he said.

"How many generation, then?" she asked.

He counted. "Four? Five?"

"Not so long, then," she said. "About a hundred years?"

"The kria are growing fewer," he said. "And the elders don't know how to stop the dying. There are too few of us to make a successful war against the humans. And now all of Waxing Moon clan is gone."

"How many died?" she asked.

He counted, converted the numbers. "One hundred and twenty-one," he said.

She caught her breath. "That many?" she asked. "Where are the rest of your people?"

He considered, but he was clear on this point, at least. "Lhassa, I cannot say," he said. "They are separated into camps, and it would be a betrayal for me to tell you where they are."

"Is that what the torture was about?" she asked. "They wanted to know where your people were?"

"Maybe some of it," he said. "But they didn't know I understood their language until you spoke to me. Perhaps they thought it was witchcraft that caused me to answer you."

She lifted her eyebrows and sighed at that.

"Why are you an outcast from your people, Ta Nyahl? Couldn't you stay with your uncle's clan?"

He should have hidden his face, should have been ashamed to explain such things to anyone. But the thought that it meant little to her saved his pride, and so he only stared into the fire, avoiding her eyes.

"Is it on my account?" she asked, striking too near the truth.

"No, lhassa," he said. "It is because of my own choices."

"Well, I'm glad you told me these things," she said. "The way events are going, I don't know if I can help you with any of it or not." She closed her eyes, looking pained, and touched her bruised temple. "I'm likely to end up hostage or dead myself."

It seemed an opening, and he asked again, "Will you tell me where the black weapon comes from, lhassa?"

She studied him, and he kept his eyes downcast, waiting for her decision. He waited respectfully as the silence extended, finally risked a glance at her. She was frowning, a heavy line between her brows. She caught the flicker of his eyes.

"Let me think about this," she said.

It was about how the kria elders had reacted, as if his questions had no acceptable answers.

They saddled the horses and went on southwest, climbing on the slopes of the mountain now. The terrain was noticeably steeper today, with the trees tending to evergreen. The soft pad of fallen needles cushioned the horses' hooves, making their ascent nearly silent. Wind sloughed in the branches above their heads, and sun filtered down in slated rays. Different animals inhabited the evergreen forest than the leafy woods below. They saw a variety of birds, and now and then Ta Nyahl identified the tracks of goats and foxes. Once they came on the trail of a baywolf pack, but the track was old.

One good result of the events over the last few days was that they seemed to have lost the pursuit. Still, the question of who the men were and what they wanted nagged at him. It seemed to worry Cybelle, too.

At noon they stopped to water the horses and eat a quick meal.

"Are we still being followed?" she asked.

He looked out at the forest, testing the scents, gauging the wind and the direction of shadows.

"I don't think so," he said. "We are a long way south of the usual pass now."

"What do you mean?" she asked. "How will we get back to it?"

"My uncle told me of another way across the mountains," he said. "It will be harder traveling for the horses, but it should be passable by now—this late in the spring."

"Oh," she said. "You think they'll be waiting for us at the other pass?"

He had made that mistake once. With Ta Marnie's advice, he hoped to avoid making it again.

"Yes," he said. "They know where you're going, don't they?"

She only tightened her lips, didn't answer. He thought she was still deciding what to tell him about her reasons for being here.

His uncle had told him what to expect. Just now they were able to stay off the main trails because of the open nature of the evergreen woods. The trees were growing sparser as they climbed up the slope, and soon the forest would end. On the south slope above the tree line were meadows where humans kept sheep, goats and other animals that provided the wool they wore. The grassy moors would be easier traveling than the rough northern trails, but the drawback was that there was no cover. They would be visible from further away and ran the risk of encountering herdsmen. That meant they needed to make a decision about the risks.

Chapter 12

As the day waned, Ta Nyahl looked for a sheltered location to camp. They were moving higher on the mountainside, climbing more steeply now. The elevation made it more likely someone in the valley could see a fire glow, and he was tempted to go without. Still, the nights were colder with the elevation, and warm food was a comfort, so he meant to have a fire if they could.

They stopped to rest the horses as they topped the rise of a small hill. Ta Nyahl turned in the saddle so he could look down their back trail. The shadows were closing in behind them, the cedars heavy with twilight. It made the wood seem mysterious, the dark branches hiding the secrets of who and what might be there. The wind flowed like a river down the mountain, telling him nothing.

"Lhassa," he said. "Do you think the men are still searching for us in the valley?"

She looked briefly where he did. Cybelle had said little during the day, but he had felt her eyes on him.

"I'm sure they are," she said. He thought she meant to say more, but she seemed to change her mind.

He decided that caution meant he should assume the men were still there where he had last seen them, and not so far away that they wouldn't see a fire on the mountain. He finally located a decent place to camp with high rocks rising on all sides. Not only would these hide the light of their fire, but it would also be a defensible position. The only drawback was that there was no water. It would be a dry camp.

"Will you camp here, lhassa?" he asked. "There is no water, but it will be a secure place."

"Yes," she said, looking at the rocks. "It's fine."

They unsaddled the horses and unloaded the packs, went about the chores of making camp. He dug a fire pit and piled up rocks to further hide their firelight. Then he took the mare with him to cut firewood. He rubbed down the horses and measured out grain for each while Cybelle kindled the fire and started bread to fry for their supper.

The fire played on the planes of her face as they ate, darkened the hollows of her eyes. She seemed lost in her own thoughts.

"Lhassa," he said, after a while. "Will you tell me about the men? Do they have some…sorcery to find us?"

She looked at him.

"Why do you want to know?" she asked.

"We will come to the end of the trees tomorrow," he said, "and we will be exposed on the slope of the mountain. I need to know how to make plans for travel."

"It's not sorcery," she said. "They might have used some kind of device to locate us in the woods, but I think you're right that they just know about where I am and where I'm going. They've probably offered the villagers a reward for information."

"I can avoid villages," he said, "but we may run into herders on the mountain who will say they saw us. Also, if we cross the grasslands, we will leave a trail of trampled grass that will be easy to follow."

"That would be a problem," she said.

"Then we should begin to travel at night when we leave the trees," he said. "That way we will be less likely to meet anyone—and we should stick to rocky ground. The north slope of the mountain will be hard traveling, difficult and dangerous, but it will be easier to hide our trail on that ascent. Also, there will be cover where we can hide our camp."

"I think that's a good idea," she said. "It will solve some other problems, as well."

He waited, but she didn't go on to explain what that meant.

"What will you do on the other side of the mountains?" he asked, finally.

She glanced at him, clearly uncomfortable with the questions. He needed to know the answers, though. If he were to continue to serve her, then he needed information on what she meant to do and what the dangers were.

"I'm…hoping to find someone," she said.

"Do you know where?" he asked. "Lhassa, I know nothing about the wastelands."

"I have an idea about landmarks," she said. "I think I can find where to go."

There was something else that had been bothering him.

"Lhassa," he said. "Do the men also have weapons like the one you carry?"

"I'm certain they do," she said, "or at least something similar."

That was a revelation. It meant the men following her were from wherever she had come from.

"Have you brought it from somewhere else?" he asked.

He was pressing for answers now. She considered it, sitting with her elbows on her knees. The firelight flickered, cast darker shadows on her face.

"You think it comes from off-world?" she asked finally.

"Yes," he said.

She took a breath. "Well, I won't lie to you," she said. "You already know it does."

"And you?" he asked. It was brazen. He expected anger, but he still held to his determination.

She looked at him straight, but again, it must be clear that he had already made a decision about it.

"Yes," she said. "The same."

"And why are you here?" he asked.

She didn't answer right away, seemed to consider what to say. He waited quietly and patiently. He had already pushed her for answers, and he didn't want to make her angry. That would cut off communication all together.

"Ta Nyahl," she said, finally. "Do you believe in witchcraft?"

It was an odd question, and a complex issue. He didn't think Cybelle was really a witch, or she would have handled her problems differently. He had always had a great respect for shamans, but those of his own people tended to work in the realm of the spirit, making sure that spiritual issues didn't lead to problems in one's daily life. The shamans in the human villages might be different, and he had heard that they cast curses and might have other, more practical magics.

"When I and my cousins were captured," he said, "they said a shaman found us, lhassa, through his magic."

"I'll bet," she said.

"In some ways I might believe in it," he said finally.

"Well, there's no witchcraft going on here," she said. "I'm not a witch."

"I didn't think so," he said.

"It's a complicated story," she said, and then stopped. "I shouldn't tell you, but you're right that your not knowing about it endangers our safety. There's no easy way to go about it, so I'll just go ahead."

She hugged her knees, stared into the fire.

"Your kria legends about coming down from the sky are probably right. There are ships that carry people between the stars, and ways to travel from one world to another. There was a survey of this world about a hundred human years ago that found no intelligent life on the planet. It was made by a company that does this kind of survey in the expectation it will get benefits from colonization. So the company reported they had found a habitable world. They established a claim and got a contract to bring in colonists. Also, the company reported that they meant to mine ores from what you call the wastelands. They made contracts with other companies to bring in the colonists, and to sell the ores. However, they recently discovered a very rare mineral here, so they submitted a request to move the colonists and mine the ore, which will cause significant environmental damage. I've come to verify that what's on their application is correct."

She glanced over at him then, waiting for a reply. Of course, it was a problem.

"Lhassa," he said, "You will have to explain what the words mean."

He was afraid she would refuse. She must have known he wouldn't understand, and this could be part of the reason that she hadn't told him any of it before. However, this was important to know, and he meant to work through it.

She rubbed her face. "Alright," she said. "Where did I lose you?"

"At the beginning," he said. "What is a ship?"

"Do you know what a boat is?" she asked.

"Yes," he said. "People use them to cross water."

"It's like that, only larger, and some ships carry people through the air, sometimes between worlds."

"And what is a survey?"

"It means people travel across the countryside and record what they see."

"By intelligent life you mean people?"

"Yes," she said.

"What is a company?"

"It's a group of people who get together to buy and sell things—to trade."

"In worlds?" he asked.

"Sometimes," she said. "More often it's for something like ores to make metal tools, or wool to make cloth."

He had forgotten the words after that, and she had to tell him the last part again. It took a little while before he understood the ideas. And quite a bit longer before he realized what was missing from the story.

"The company," he said, "has not mentioned the kria in this?"

There had been silence in the firelight while he thought about it. When he said that, she glanced over at him and laughed suddenly. It was something he hadn't heard her do, an expression that she had apparently had little use for during the hardship of their journey.

"No," she said. "Not a word about the kria. It's something of a major problem for their application."

"Why is that, lhassa?" he asked. "Couldn't the company contract to move the kria as well as the humans?"

"Well," she said, "they might have tried to do that, but apparently they've decided on genocide instead. The problem is that the kria have been here for nearly a hundred years. That means your people have a claim to the world through what is called adverse possession."

"What is genocide?" he asked.

"Offering a bounty for dead kria."

He considered that.

"If you've come from a ship," he asked finally, "how did you end up in the forest?"

"I work for the government," she said. "The agency I work for sent a team here to evaluate the company's application."

The words were unfamiliar—she had lost him again.

"What is 'government' and what is 'agency'?" he asked.

"A government is like the village headman," she said, "and a council of elders, except on a larger scale. An agency is a group of people working for the government that has a specific purpose."

"And there is a team that came with you?" he asked.

"Yes," she said. "Another person—a man. That's why I'm trying to get back across the mountains. The company has a base there, and I need to find my partner in this again."

She rocked a little, rubbed at her face.

"The company's application looked fine on the surface," she said. "It's all very reasonable, and supported by surveys and statistics—that is, numbers. Because the application looked well done, there's was a temptation to take it at face value. But I wanted to be thorough. I thought it was important. If the application is approved, they'll turn this world into a cinder. So, once we got here, something bothered me about the way the company employees behaved. There was a manager and a group of employees that met us and showed us around the mining camps in the wastelands, but they didn't seem very willing to let us look around in the villages."

She touched her chin, where a bruise must still hurt, brushed back a wisp of hair.

"They said this was because the villagers were primitive," she said, "and that contact with off-world technology would contaminate their environment, but I knew they had contact with the villagers already. I asked to come across the mountains and have a look, maybe talk with some of the villagers. They put me off for a while, but I insisted. Eventually, I got a trip scheduled in one of the company's flyers and a couple of employees to come along and show me around.

"We started out early, before first light. I saw a fire in the forest as soon as we crossed the mountains."

"At the Tanner village?" he asked.

"Yes," she said. "That's where it was. How do you know?"

"My cousins and I set it," he said. "We piled brush and wood against the palisade during the night and set fire to it."

"Ah," she said. "And they caught you?"

"Yes," he said. "They were very angry about it."

"I can see why," she said. "It looked like you caused a lot of damage in the village. Several of the huts caught fire and burned, some of the storehouses. Anyway, I saw the fire, and I asked to stop and see what was going on. The pilot refused—and that made me even more suspicious.

"We went on down the coast. I got a count of the villages, checked the estimates of population. We landed at a fishing village pretty far to the south and I talked with some of the people there. When we came back north, though, I insisted that we check and see what the fire was about. I wanted to land at the Tanner village.

"We argued about it, and finally the pilot set down in a clearing a little distance away. They said we could walk to the village from there. It took a few minutes for us to get started, and I wasn't suspecting anything, but the two of them turned on me suddenly. I wouldn't have gotten away from them except for a bear—is it called a las?"

"Yes," he said. "Very large and fierce?'

"That's it," she said. "When they saw it, they let go of me and took off back to the flyer."

She tightened her arms around her knees and rocked again, staring into the fire.

"I didn't know what to do, so I started off to walk to the village," she said. "I ran into a boy, maybe ten years old, that the bear had cornered. I fired at it with my weapon and killed it. The boy was scratched and bruised, but not really badly hurt. He took me to the village and told his father I was a witch who had saved him. Tanner offered me whatever I wanted in return.

"So I thought, 'I'll ask for horses and supplies and maybe I can get back to the base,' but I didn't know how hard it would be. Plus," she said, "you know I got you as part of the bargain."

"Yes," he said.

She closed her eyes, took a breath. In that moment, he could clearly see the burdened woman underneath her calm exterior.

"I'm in serious trouble," she admitted. "There's a lot at stake with the application—a lot of income riding on it. I think they meant to kill me and make it seem like an accident. I don't think those are search parties to rescue me in the woods—they're likely murder squads instead. I want to get back to the base on my own and back with my partner without them knowing."

"Can you do that, lhassa?" he asked.

"I have to," she said. "There's the added problem of your people now, and the genocide. I can't do anything about any of it unless I can get to the communications equipment at the base. I'll need to send off a report right away and to ask for help. I'm hoping that will guarantee our safety."

The words flowed past him. He was understanding what she said reasonably well since she had taken the time to explain—but he was still grappling with the implications. It was no surprise that there had been treachery at work in the human business of the application. He didn't understand what she meant to do about it, though.

"What is communications equipment?" he asked. "What do you mean 'send off a report'?"

"Off-world humans have a lot of technology," she said. "That means very advanced tools like the flyers and the weapon I have. There are also ways to send messages at a distance—even back to the agency where I work on a different world. I need to send a message to them about what's going on. Once it's done, then kidnapping or killing me won't do very much good."

"Ah," he said.

"At least," she said. "I hope not."

He thought that meant she didn't have any idea how far the treachery went.

The matter of the communication over a distance explained a lot. He would have to think carefully about how they should make their way through the mountain pass. If their pursuers had flyers so they could soar like birds and ways to send messages over a distance, then there were serious dangers about leaving the cover of the forest.

He took the first watch because he wanted to think about what Cybelle had told him. She rolled in her blankets and seemed to fall sleep immediately—likely still hurting and exhausted from wandering in the woods without horses or supplies.

He let her sleep until the first moon set, and then he wakened her for the second watch. He rolled in his own blankets and slept heavily, too. He wasn't that far from exhaustion himself. It would take a while for the recent hardships to wear off.

Cybelle woke him as the small moon rose, and they had a quick meal, saddled the horses and set off up the mountain. The sky was clear after the rain, and the moonlight was bright enough that he felt safe enough even on the rough and rocky north slopes of the peak. They walked much of the way, leading the horses, and he picked a safe path with his better night sight.

As the sky began to pale toward dawn, he found another sheltered site in the rocks where they could spend the day. The heavy forest below had given way here to sparse undergrowth and a few stunted evergreens. This time, he was careful to find a spot overhung by cliffs to protect them from unfriendly eyes that might pass overhead.

The horses seemed grateful they had stopped. The shift to night travel meant they'd had less rest than usual, and the way was steep. Ta Nyahl unsaddled them and measured out a ration of grain. The mare was even civil when he rubbed her down with dried grass and bent to clean her feet with a stick.

While he was working, Cybelle built a small fire with dry wood from the packs and fried bread and meat for a morning meal. Heavy smoke might give them away, but the dry wood made very little, and he thought it would be safe enough.

Cybelle took the first watch this time, and he rolled in his blankets and slept soundly. She woke him about noon and took her own opportunity to sleep. While she slept, he climbed higher into the rocks, found a place where he could look out over the forest they had left below. From this height on the mountain, he could just see the blue of the sea and how it curved into the horizon. The strip of fertile land between the sea and the mountains was home for the kria as well as for the humans who lived there, and he tried to imagine what Cybelle had said about the humans' plans to destroy it.

This world had always been a difficult place for the kria to live in, but still it was a fair world, very beautiful in its way. It had a bounty of fish and game that provided for all who had a place in the valley. He wondered that the company men meant to kill all the kria so they could destroy the world without opposition. That was what he had taken from what Cybelle said. Not only that, they were determined enough that they meant to capture and maybe kill her in order to go on with the work. It seemed very evil.

He wished he had the council of elders to help him think through what he should do with this information. He reached up and touched the warrior's knot braided at the nape of his neck. Sa Rahn had said he was the only warrior left for Waxing Moon. He remembered, too, what Ka Tehnie had said about doing what he could for the future. The hard question was what that might be. All he could think of now was to help Cybelle Lawton in her efforts to send off her report.

As the sky began to color with sunset, he descended the rocky trail to the spot where he had left Cybelle and the horses. She was already stirring, rolling her blankets to pack away.

"Have you been up in the rocks?" she asked.

"Yes," he said.

"Could you see anything?"

"I may have seen one of the flyers," he said. "There was something to the north that didn't look like a hawk."

She glanced up at him. "I wouldn't be surprised," she said.

He built up the little fire again, and she got out cured meat, onions and flour to make bread.

"Should I make extra bread?" she asked. "Will we be able to have a fire in the morning?"

"I think it would be well," he said. "We'll be more exposed as we go higher, and tonight we will run into snow.

If we can't find cover, we won't be able to have a fire—they will see it from below."

"How long before we reach the pass?" she asked.

"If we make good time, we may go through it early in the morning," he said. "But higher on the mountain, the snow drifts may get deep and slow us down. I've never been this way, but I asked about it in the kria camp. My uncle said that we should take much care."

They ran into scattered patches of snow before the first moon rose, and by midnight a pack of baywolves was following them. Ta Nyahl caught their scent in an eddy of wind, stopped to look back along their trail.

"What is it?" asked Cybelle.

They were walking though ankle deep snow cover, leading the horses along a rocky ledge.

"Baywolves," he said.

It was unusual for kria to have problems with predators, likely because their own scent was a warning. Now he had the woman and the horses with him, though, and the baywolves were tracking them across the snow.

"Are they dangerous?" she asked.

"They can be," he said.

"Should we do anything?" she asked.

"Not yet," he said. He couldn't see the wolves behind them, so he turned and resumed the ascent. As they got closer to the pass, they would probably have to use the trail, but for now he was staying off it, trying to keep to the rocks where they would be harder to track. Because of what Cybelle had told him about the flyers, he thought the sign they left behind them should be hidden as much as possible. If flyers could identify them or their track, then someone would come to investigate. Once onto the trail, trackers from the village could find them as easily as the humans' technology.

The snow was crisp and cold, at least two days old. They made steady progress up the mountain, and he began to look for a way to the pass. They were a little south of the ram formation where the gap cut through the mountain. Once they were in the snowfields their track would show over open ground, regardless, but he wanted to keep to rock or undergrowth as much as possible.

As the night wore on, they ran into heavier snow drifts and their progress slowed. They had to spend a lot of time in breaking a trail. The work was tiring, and as they slowed, the wolves closed the distance between them. Now they could hear the yips that signaled the pack was hunting. Rather than be caught on the crest of the mountain in daylight, Ta Nyahl decided to look for a place to stop. As the last moon set, he found a sheltered spot against a cliff face, almost a crevice, that was nearly clear of snow.

"Lhassa," he said to Cybelle, "We will be caught in the daylight. Will you stop here?"

"Stop," she said from behind the mare. She sounded faint and weary.

Chapter 13

Ta Nyahl saw to the horses, but this time he didn't settle by the fire afterwards. Instead, he circled the camp, leaving his scent and marking it as his territory. When he got back to the fire, the sky had paled with dawn and Cybelle had their breakfast cooking.

He was finishing up his bowl when Cybelle said in a tense voice, "Ta Nyahl..."

He knew they were there, but he turned to look. The pack of baywolves was loping up the slope along their back trail. They were big animals with fierce eyes and heavy fangs. They had broad feet for running on the snow, and their shaggy coats were nearly as white as the drifts.

"They should stop," he said. Just in case they didn't, he got up and strung his bow.

The pack charged up the hill until they reached the ring he had made in the snow, and then they did stop, as he had expected. The mixed scents of the trail had confused them, but the circle he had made around the camp was a clear warning. Regardless of their civilization, the kria had not lost their understanding of scents and markings, and predators respected their property.

The baywolves milled in confusion, yapping and howling. He watched them for a while, but none of the pack seemed bold enough to cross into his territory. They bristled as he stared at them, and one or two snarled.

"What should we do?" asked Cybelle.

"Nothing," he said. "I'll take the first watch."

She looked at him oddly, but his surety must have soothed her worry. She rolled into her blankets and went to sleep with the wolves still circling and snapping in the pale dawn light.

The pack made a decision about what to do about mid-morning, and withdrew back down the slope. Ta Nyahl hoped they had given up following, but the animals were thin and ravenous at the end of winter, and he thought they might continue to trail the party, perhaps hoping to get at one of the horses.

The sun rose into a clear sky, and glint off the snow was nearly blinding. A soft cloud lay in the valley below that obscured the forest and sea coast, as well. After the wolves disappeared, there was no sound but the wind flirting through the rocks behind him. It was a cold and lonely sound, as if he were truly alone.

He slept soundly in the afternoon while Cybelle stood watch, but heavy clouds had come up while he slept, and damp had crept into his bones. His shoulder ached, and by the time he woke, he was stiff and nearly shivering.

The fire helped, as did a full belly. They saddled the horses and lashed on the packs, and then sat for a while as the small blaze died down to embers, trying to absorb what they could of its warmth before the sun set. The stars began to come out in the darkening sky, the bright blue and gold evening stars clearly visible in the last pale, unclouded strip of sky to the west.

"Lhassa," he said. "Will you tell me where you came from? Is it one of the stars we can see from here?"

"I don't think so," she said. "It's a long way off."

He spread his hands to catch the heat from the dying coals.

"How did you come here?" he asked. "On one of the ships?"

She rubbed her face and frowned, as if she was uncomfortable in talking about it.

"Part of the way," she said, finally. "There's something called a wormhole bridge that lets you travel from one place to the other very quickly, and then we took a small ship from a station in the sky to the surface of the world here."

"Are there villages on your world?" he asked.

"Yes, but most people live in larger settlements called cities. They have buildings like the villagers' huts, but bigger and better built. There's a lot of technology—machines, that would seem like sorcery to someone from this world."

"And you do work for an…agency?" he asked.

"Yes," she said. "It regulates commerce, tries to make sure people are treated fairly."

"Do you trust the people you work for?" he asked.

"Yes," I do," she said. "I think they make a real effort for fairness, and…also to make sure people get justice who have been wronged. Speaking of that…" She sighed. "Ta Nyahl," she said. "I think I need to apologize for the human race."

Her voice sounded wry and bitter, and he glanced up. She looked angry about it, and he dropped his eyes quickly, giving her privacy for her emotion. He didn't want to destroy the flow of her words.

"I want you to know that all humans don't conduct themselves this way," she said. "There really are some good people out there."

He found nothing to say in response. He had learned a lot about humans in recent days, and this was one of the things that he had come to wonder about. The wind gusted, making its cold, fluting song in the rocks. From somewhere, a fox yipped.

He took a breath.

"How would the kria make a claim to this world?" he asked. "Is it something the elders would have to do?"

Cybelle's eyes flickered over to him. For a long moment she didn't say anything, but then she smiled faintly. He thought she might be considering her words carefully.

"No," she said, finally. "One person is enough. You should file a complaint about the genocide, too."

"How is it done?" he asked.

"When I file my report, I can tell them you want to do it," she said. "I'm pretty sure the agency can handle it for you. We just have to get safely to the base to do it."

That was something he had meant to arrange, anyway—if there was any way he could.

"What shall I do at your base when we get there?" he asked. "What will I do about my oath to you?"

She tightened her lips at that. The dying light left her nearly a silhouette against the sunset, but he could see the question troubled her.

"That's a problem," she said. "My people don't take slaves, regardless of what the custom is here. I don't know what to do about this…relationship. I'm grateful for your help, Ta Nyahl, but I need for you to know you're not really obligated to me in any way."

It meant that she did mean to abandon him, he thought. She only wanted to get back to her people, and then he would be on his own. It didn't really matter, though, as long as he accomplished what he wanted. It seemed she would handle that much for him, at least.

By the time they were ready to go, it was flurrying snow. They doused the fire, and as full dark fell, mounted and set off through a swirl of flakes toward the gap in the peaks above. The snow flew sideways on the wind, lowering visibility. That made it more of a risk in moving out of the rocky terrain and onto the trail that led through the pass—the cliff face was very steep on the downhill side. There was no other way through the gap, though. They made steady progress. After a while, Ta Nyahl turned and looked back along their trail. One of the wolves was still following them.

"What is it?" asked Cybelle. She wiped the snow out of her eyes, turned to look backward.

"A wolf," he said. "It must be starving."

Instinct had warned him. He strung his bow again, checked to make sure the arrows were loose in the quiver. He glimpsed it in a little while—an old wolf with a thin, straggly coat. It wouldn't be fast or agile enough to catch most game in the mountains. The horses and the woman were just too much temptation.

"Lhassa, change places with me," he said to Cybelle.

"What?" she asked.

"Come here and take the mare," he said. "I'll walk behind."

She came past him, the snow lying white on her hair. They tethered the bay to the mare and Cybelle led off through the snow, stumbling now and then in the darkness. He heard her curse, but he didn't turn to look. He was watching their back trail.

The wolf followed steadily, gaining on them. Ta Nyahl thought it would break off once it scented him, but it didn't. That meant there would be trouble. He stopped and unslung the bow from around his shoulder, reached back and tugged an arrow from the quiver.

He was unsure of his shoulder. He had successfully drawn the bow when he tried it in the woods, but he knew he couldn't hold the draw for very long. Still, it was better than trying to fend off the wolf with just a knife.

He nocked the arrow and waited. The wolf slowed as he stopped. It was only a few spans away now. It lowered its head and snarled at him. The faint light outlined the dark shape, flashed on the exposed fangs. Behind him, Cybelle cried out something. He hardly heard it. He was focused on the wolf, watching its body language, testing its scent.

When it charged, he drew the bow and let the arrow fly in the same motion. He knew one arrow wouldn't stop it. He dodged to the side, stumbled in a drift and almost fell. He caught his balance, loosed another arrow. The bay horse screamed and bucked, jerked at its tether. The mare jumped sideways, floundered in a drift. The wolf dropped this time, rolled in the snow.

Cybelle was there beside him then, her weapon in her hand.

Ta Nyahl had nocked another arrow, but now he let it fall. He reached and caught her hand.

"Wait!" he said. "Will it make fire?"

"Ah," she said. "I didn't think…" She dropped her hand.

She was too late, anyway. The wolf was down, its dark blood flowing on the snow.

Ta Nyahl took a deep breath, rubbed at his shoulder. It ached like fire where the healing muscles had been overstrained. The arm had worked well enough, though. He pulled out his knife, stepped in and cut the wolf's throat. It would bleed to death if he just left it, but he meant to take away its pain.

Once it was completely dead, he cut out his arrows, cleaned them and put them back into the quiver—they were well made and too valuable to just leave. Then he dragged the carcass into the cover of brush a little distance below them. He began to scoop snow over the blood on their trail, and Cybelle realized what he was doing, helped him cover it over. He didn't want it to be visible once the sun rose in the morning.

They didn't have to worry about the carcass. It had no marks of Cybelle's weapon on it, and predators would take care of it quickly enough—maybe before morning. The horses waited a little distance above them on the slope, nervous at the scent of blood, but calm enough now. They went on.

The snowfall died finally. The field before them was very white, a soft glow lighting the darkness so it was easy to see the way. The drifts further up the mountain had already been broken by what looked to be goats moving on the game track. Once they were on it, traveling was easier. They made good progress and soon crossed to the other side of the crags. Strangely, there was moonlight here. When he looked back, Ta Nyahl could see the heavy snow clouds lying in the pass—blocked by the peak from flowing through.

As soon as the trail began to incline downward, Ta Nyahl looked for a way to hide their tracks. He bore to the north again, found brush and rocks that would give them cover. The snow was knee-deep here, and he had to break trail again. Still, he thought the slow progress was better than leaving a clear track down the mountain for someone to see from the air.

They labored on through the night, and by the time the sky began to pale, the snow cover was thinning. They found a place to camp in heavy brush this time, and didn't risk a fire. As the sun rose, Ta Nyahl took the first watch, and looked out on a different world.

The wastelands were bare and rocky, the lush forest on the other side of the mountains replaced by scrubby brush. The soil looked red from this height. Flat plains stretched to a misty, purple distance and another range of mountains. To the south he caught a glimmer of light.

It wasn't firelight, he thought. Instead of the warm flicker that would be a campfire, it was a line of static lights that he couldn't interpret. As the sunlight grew stronger, the lights went out. He thought about it for a while, and then remembered what Cybelle had said about the humans' technology. It might be the base she was looking for. If it was, then he knew where they were going.

"Will they expect you to come to the base?" he asked Cybelle, as they finished up another breakfast of cheese and cold, fried bread.

"Of course, they know where I'm headed," she said. "But they won't know we've crossed the mountain, will they?"

It was a good thought that his care in hiding their trail might have paid off. His mistake that had endangered them in the woods had brought him great shame, and he had resolved not to be caught again. He had worked harder at hiding their track, and now he hoped the men were still trying to unsnarl the puzzle he had left them in the valley on the other side of the mountain.

The decent down the slope had its own dangers, but progress was faster than the trip up. The snow here was lighter. The sky was clear on this side of the mountain, the clouds and unruly weather seemingly trapped on the other side of the peak. The moons gave a clear light, and the way was relatively easy. The bay horse followed close behind the mare, and for once, seemed surefooted.

They left the snow by the time the first moon rose, and continued downward toward the foothills. There was no cover in the wastelands to hide them from view, but the dry, rocky soil and scrubby vegetation meant their trail could be more easily hidden than in the snow. They could solve the visibility problem by continuing to travel during the night. Ta Nyahl took care to keep off the game trails and to backtrack and otherwise work to confuse a tracker. It was the best he could do in the strange countryside.

It was harder to find a place to camp when they descended into the foothills, as the scrubby brush offered little cover. In the first light of dawn, Ta Nyahl finally found a place against a rock cliff with stunted trees growing at the base, and behind it a cave. He thought it must be a kindness sent by his predecessors, as they were out of bread and getting low on cheese and dried meat. They needed a fire to cook tonight.

The cave wasn't large enough for the horses. He bent to go inside and check, found the space was bare and empty. Cat scent lay on the debris—a panther, he thought—but it was old. Luck was with them today—there was a trickle of water within the cavern that dribbled into a small pool. It tasted heavily of minerals, but it was good enough. He went back out to where Cybelle was waiting with the horses.

"Come inside, lhassa," he said. "This is a good place."

It was a luxury after the days of cold, dry camps on the mountain. They hadn't suffered for water because of the snow, but now they needed to fill the water skins again. Tough bunches of grass grew under the trees, but there looked to be little moisture in it. The dry soil meant the horses would need more water than in the forest.

Ta Nyahl broke off some of the tough grass to rub down the horses, then measured out feed and tethered them to graze for a while. By then Cybelle had a small campfire built inside the mouth of the cave and was frying bread and onions. He sat by the fire.

"Your base is to the south?" he asked.

"Yes," she said.

"I saw it from the mountain," he said. "We should be there sometime tomorrow night."

She turned the bread in the skillet, looked over at him.

"Are you sure it's so close? The dry air can be deceptive."

He considered. "I think so, lhassa. We are further south than we otherwise would be, because of the way we took over the mountain. We will come out of the hills tonight, and we should make good progress across the flat land. Speed may help us more now than trying to hide our track."

Cybelle tightened her lips. "Then I'll have to make some plans for getting us in," she said.

"Will there be a palisade?" he asked.

"A fence," she said. "It's about the same thing, but it may be harder to get past."

She took the first watch, and he woke at midday to sit in the cave entrance and watch the bare, empty terrain outside. Light and shadow flowed over the landscape, shifting its features. The air heated up with the sun, brought scents that suggested the countryside wasn't as empty as it looked. He tested the wind as it gusted and turned, learning about it. There was game here, and likely more hidden springs like the one in the cavern. It was pleasant in the shade of the trees, and the horses dozed quietly. There were no signs of danger.

It was there, regardless, he thought. There were huge risks in what they were planning to do. He was already a long way from home, and now he was going into a different world— one held by the enemy. Once inside the humans' fence, he would be trapped. He was relying on Cybelle's belief that she could keep them safe inside. If that wasn't so, then there would be little he could do against humans with the kind of weapons she carried. Most likely he would be dead in the first hostile encounter.

But there was a lot at stake here—more than he would ever have dreamed. If he understood Cybelle correctly, this whole world was in danger, and not just the kria. It felt like unreality—like a dream—to look out at the red plains and purple mountains and think that humans meant to destroy it just for the wealth it would bring them. Cybelle said they meant to move the human population, but they had made no plans to save anything else. He tried to imagine the world as a cinder the way Cybelle had described it—the green forests burnt away, the birds and foxes dead, the sky sere and empty and the sea only a dead puddle lapping at a silent shore. The vision was horrific. He closed his eyes and shuddered at the very idea.

Ta Nyahl woke Cybelle at sunset. As they waited for their breakfast to fry, he watched the shadow of the first moon grow brighter in the sky. It was waning, and only a ragged crescent marked its progress through the dusk. The night wind was cold here, even though they had left the snowline well behind them. Ta Nyahl pulled his woolen cloak tighter around his shoulders, shivered slightly in the chill. In the distance he heard a baywolf howl.

"Lhassa," he asked, "have you decided how we can get in? What kind of defenses will the base have?"

"The fence is made of wire," she said. "If they've not changed the security code, I can get us through the gate. If they've changed it… I'm not sure. We'll have to decide when we get there."

"Are there sentries?"

The bread sizzled in the pan. She checked the underside of one of the cakes, lifted the skillet off the fire.

"No," she said. She frowned. "I've been thinking about it. I'm sure there are security cameras that would let them see someone coming," she said. "But they're not expecting an attack, so I doubt if anyone will be monitoring the feeds in the middle of the night. There are sonics to keep animals away from the fence. As long as we don't set off an alarm, then I think we might be able to ride right up to the gate."

She handed him a bowl of stew and the bread, took hers in her lap to eat.

"It's unprotected?" he asked.

"Not quite," she said. "There's probably some kind of signal that transmits when it opens—an alarm. The question is, what kind."

"What do you mean?" he asked.

"Whether it's something that would wake them up to come check, or whether there's just a notice that it happened."

He thought about it. The humans must have no expectation that they would be attacked. The base was very isolated here in the wastelands, and it sounded like the defenses were only to keep animals or chance intruders out of the grounds. If they had no idea that Cybelle had crossed the mountains and was nearly at the gate, then they might not have set any watch at all.

"So they may have no defenses other than the fence?" he asked.

She laughed suddenly. It was a harsh, dark sound.

"Maybe not," she said. "I hope they've seriously underestimated the threat."

That seemed unbelievably lax—but these were humans with weapons like Cybelle's. They might not really have any care who rode up to their gate. The reasons for that made him wonder again about the risks.

There seemed no more to say about it, though. He had finished up his meal. He got up and lifted the skillet, ready to take it for cleaning.

"Ta Nyahl," said Cybelle, "wait a minute."

He stopped.

"There are some things we need to talk about," she said. Her face seemed very serious. "Sit back down, please."

He put the skillet down and took his seat again, watched as she turned her bowl in her hands. He sat patiently, waiting while she found the words.

"I need to let you know that I don't know what will happen at the base," she said finally. "I need your help, but I don't know if I can protect us…if I can protect you…Do you understand what I mean?"

He looked down at the skillet. This was what he had been thinking about himself. That meant he wasn't unprepared to talk about it.

"What do you think about it, lhassa?"

She stared up at the fading colors of the sky.

"There will be cameras that record our image when we come up to the gate. I don't think they will know we're there until morning, but it means they *will* know. So, once we ride up to the gate, then we're exposed. There's not much cover in this wilderness to hide from a search. If you don't want to take the risks, then you should leave me and go back over the mountains now."

He thought about it.

"Then you would try to go on alone and send your report?"

"Yes," she said.

He understood the problem. "But I wouldn't be able to make the complaint about genocide?" he asked. "Or make a claim to this world?"

"That's right," she said. "I could report what I've seen, but you would have to be there to do that."

"And then what, lhassa? What happens after your report is sent?"

"I don't know. I can ask my agency to send someone to help us, but I don't know how long it would take for them to get here. We'll be on our own for a while."

So, she meant he had to be willing to die for it. Dying was something he had been expecting since last year— he had been on the edge of it for a long time. If he went back over the mountains now, he might only delay it for a little while.

"Lhassa, I will go to the base with you," he said.

"You're sure?" she asked. "You understand that it will be very dangerous. I think my life is in danger, too. We might both end up dying."

"But you're still going?"

Her eyes seemed very dark in the firelight. The bruises on her face made a shadowy pattern of uncertainty.

"I don't have any other choice," she said. "I have to do something. If I can't get to that communications equipment,

I'm stuck. It will be only a matter of time before they find me."

So, the prospect of dying was the same for her as it was for him. It seemed an odd circumstance that had brought them to this point.

"I will go to the base with you," he said.

"You're sure?" she asked.

"I have nothing to go back to."

She took a deep breath, let it out slowly. Behind her, the light was dying. The bright first stars of evening were glowing into existence above her head.

"Well," she said. She tightened her lips. "The fatalism is a bit depressing, but I'm glad to have you along. Listen," she went on, "I need to thank you for—your faithfulness in this. You've done a great job against the odds to get me here."

He glanced up at her, found her face was very grave. He had a response for her thanks this time.

"Thank you," he said, "for trying to help."

After all, she could have just let the world end.

Chapter 14

They packed up their supplies then, and Ta Nyahl saddled the horses. As he handed Cybelle the bay's reins, he felt a tremor run through her hands. Her scent gave away nervousness, but there was nothing of fear. She was a brave woman, he thought, to plan this kind of foray and have no fear.

They mounted and rode off as full darkness fell. The cameras at the gate would know they were there soon, so Ta Nyahl stopped trying to hide their sign, only kept the horses to a steady pace southwest. Just after midnight he caught the glimmer of light from the base. It almost looked like a moonrise, but none of the moons rose in the southwest.

He reined the mare to a stop, waited for Cybelle's bay to come alongside.

He pointed out the dim glow of light. "Lhassa," he said. "Is that it?"

"Yes," she said. "There's nothing else out here that would be lighted."

"We should be there by the second moon rise," he said.

"That soon?" she asked. She pulled her jacket closer in the chill air. "We should take care, then. I don't want to run into any surprises."

He slowed the mare's pace slightly and made sure to test the wind. The air was stagnant in the still of the night, and the scents had pooled in the basin. Within a little while, he caught scent of the place, men and horses, and other things he didn't recognize. The pooling of scent made it hard to judge accurately, but he thought their approach was safe enough. As Cybelle had said, there seemed to be no human sentries.

The eastern horizon lightened with the rise of the second moon, and by its light he could see the fence clearly. Worse than that, he could hear a high-pitched keening sound that set his teeth on edge. He shook his head, covered his ears.

Cybelle looked at him.

"The sonics…" she said.

"You can't hear it?" he asked.

"No," she said. "They're meant to keep animals away from the gate."

"Ah," he said. "It hurts." He took a breath, dropped his hands. "Maybe it will be alright."

The whining got worse as the got nearer the fence, but it wasn't anything he couldn't endure. It made his teeth ache, though, left him in distress so it was hard to concentrate on what they were doing. As a defense system, it was curious, but maybe effective. If someone had been waiting for them, he might have missed them, considering the noise in his ears. Just in itself, though, it wouldn't stop him from getting through the fence.

Cybelle seemed correct that they could ride right up to the gate. Looking at it close up—and at the fence, he was surprised to see that it was made completely of metal, woven into a kind of open mesh. At the top were strands of wire that seemed barbed. Beyond it were the buildings she'd said would be there, about a length away in a lighted yard.

Cybelle dismounted, walked up to the gate. There was a square plate on it where she touched lighted keys, but nothing happened.

"They've changed the security code," she said quietly "I should have realized they would."

"You can't get it to open?" he asked.

"No," she said.

He thought about it. The gate was stout enough to hold against animals, but it wasn't much of a barrier to someone who was really determined.

"We can pull it down," he said. "The horses can do it."

She looked at him. He waited for her decision.

"Alright," she said. She lifted her shoulders in a shrug. She sounded worried, but her determination was still solid.

"I was hoping to do this without damage," she said. "It may set off an alarm, but we're not that far from where I need to go. We'll probably get there regardless."

"What will happen if an alarm wakes them?" he asked.

"They're probably all asleep now," she said. She pushed her hair back out of her eyes. "It's late, and someone will have to get up and get dressed, come out to see what the problem is. We'll see the lights come on in the buildings."

"You were hoping they wouldn't know?"

"Ah," she said. "Not until the morning, anyway. They'll know we've come in as soon as they check the security footage."

He considered what she had said about damage. The obvious thing was to tie a rope around the gatepost and anchor it to the mare's saddle—she could likely pull the gate down in a single jerk. Instead, he studied the lock in the moonlight, thought he understood where the latch was under the plate.

"Lhassa," he said. "Is this the latch?"

"Yes," she said. "That's it."

He fastened the rope there, and the mare snapped it off as soon as the rope pulled taut. The gate swung open, and there was no alarm that he could hear. It was all very quiet, and there was no damage to anything but the latch.

"Wonderful," said Cybelle quietly. "Let's go."

They rode the horses through the opening, and Ta Nyahl pushed it closed again, tied it back together with a piece of leather thong around the gate posts. Looking back at it, he thought it looked almost undisturbed. If someone were to pass by, they might not notice anything was amiss. The whining in his ears reduced as they got further away from the gate. He took a long, breath as it finally faded, let it out in relief.

They rode in quietly along a wide road, aiming toward the lights in the yard. There were several large buildings and a few smaller sheds within the fence. Through some miracle, breaking open the gate didn't seem to have disturbed the camp, at all. Except for the security lights on the poles, it all seemed quiet and sleeping. It was clear that these humans, even more so than the villagers across the mountains, had a very casual approach to their security. The kria would never have been caught like this without sentries.

The silent invasion suited his instincts, the kria urge to move on quiet feet, to fade into the darkness and shadows.

He was far more comfortable with it than Cybelle, who still smelled of worry—even though she was in familiar territory now.

He didn't know where they were going, so he followed close behind the woman. She reined her bay off toward the rightmost building, near the fence on that side. All the structures stood off the ground on posts, with a dark space underneath. The walls were very straight and true and seemed to be made of wood. The roofs were peaked. There were openings in the walls that seemed filled with dark, clear sheets that moved like water—the light glinted off them. He identified doorways that were filled with wooden panels and apparently locked with the same kind of plate that had been on the gate.

Cybelle stopped the bay horse at the building, dismounted. She climbed two steps and tried the plate. The lighted symbols flowed across it, but it looked like her efforts failed again.

"Well, damn," she said.

When she turned and came back down the steps, he could see her lips were tight.

"Wait," she said. "I can get Dixon to let us in."

She got back on the bay horse, and he followed her around to the side of the building that faced the fence.

"Hopefully he's still sleeping in the same room he was," she said quietly. "I'll tap on the window and wake him up to let us in."

From the back of the horse, she could reach the windows easily enough. She counted them off, reached up to tap on one of the panes. At first nothing happened, and she rapped harder. A light came on inside where she had tapped. It was unexpected, and Ta Nyahl blinked, started. The mare snorted and sidestepped.

"Shh," said Cybelle. "Keep the horse quiet." She tapped at the window again.

The window moved outward.

"Is this some kind of joke?" said a man's voice. "It's the middle of the night."

"Dixon," the woman said, "It's Cybelle. Open the door for me."

"Cybelle?" he said.

"Shh," she said again. "Keep it quiet, please. The security code is changed. Come let me in. Don't turn on the lights."

He hesitated, apparently full of questions, but he didn't ask them.

"Alright," he said.

The window closed again and the light went out.

"Let's go," Cybelle said, and led off toward the doorway.

When they got to it, it was open this time, and the man Dixon was waiting on the step. He was clear enough to Ta Nyahl in the dim light, a tall man with dusky skin and short, dark hair. He was wearing a white shirt and short pants that he must have been sleeping in.

"Cybelle," he said, "where have you…"

"Shh." She cut him off. "Let us in, and then we can talk."

There was no hitching post for the horses, but there was a rail along the side of the building where they could loop the reins. Ta Nyahl made sure they were tied, but then he hesitated.

Cybelle must have sensed his uncertainty. She reached out and caught his sleeve, pulled him after her. He climbed the steps behind her, passed through the doorway. She closed the door behind them, leaned against it. He heard her breath go out.

"What's going on?" asked the man Dixon. "Where the hell have you been for two weeks?"

"Trying to get back here," she said. Her voice was clear now, all business. "Dixon, we are in serious trouble here. The application is lacking in some very important information, and we are at risk because I've found it out."

"What happened?" he said. "The flyer pilot, Jamison, said you'd wandered away into the woods. They've been searching everywhere for you."

"I didn't wander away," she said. "Jamison and Hendrix attacked me, and God only knows what would have happened except for a bear. They've lied on the application." She pushed away from the door. "Is the equipment on?" she asked. "I need to file a report now, before anyone finds out I'm back here. I'm going to deny the application. If you have any input, let me have it now."

She moved away from the wall, stopped, turned. It wasn't completely dark inside the building. There was a dim glow from somewhere low that lighted the room, outlined her figure.

"Wait," she said. "I need to introduce you. This is Ta Nyahl. Ta Nyahl, this is my partner Dixon Thomas."

The man looked at him, back at her.

"I don't understand. Have you brought one of the villagers back with you?" he asked.

"Dixon," she said. "He's not a human."

There was silence for a moment, and then the man said, "What?"

"There's another intelligent species living on this planet."

"Oh, lord," he said.

"One of the things they left out of the application. Ta Nyahl," she went on, "would you wait here for a few minutes? You can sit down in one of the chairs and get comfortable. It will take me a little while to do the report. I'll let you know when I need you."

She turned then, and headed back toward where Dixon had been sleeping. The man glanced at Ta Nyahl uncertainly, then followed close behind her.

"Cybelle," he said to her, "you're not supposed to make contact with alien races."

The man was upset. He had pitched his voice so he thought Ta Nyahl wouldn't hear, but his ears were sharp, caught the words clearly as they walked up the passageway.

"It was an accident," she said. "In the dark, I couldn't tell what he was."

"Then you should have withdrawn," he said.

"There were issues," she said. "I'll just have to deal with it."

The two of them went down the short passage and disappeared through a doorway. Ta Nyahl shifted to see where they went, caught a glimmer of witch light from inside the room. He blinked and shivered when he saw it, thinking of magic, but then he remembered what Cybelle had said about there being no magic here. It must only be her equipment.

He glanced around the room where she had told him to wait. There was nothing familiar here. It was filled with strange objects that looked to be crafted. She had said to sit down, so he decided some of the things must be meant to sit on—they seemed shaped vaguely like stools. He sat on one experimentally; found it was springy and comfortable enough. He had never seen furnishings like this. Some of the other objects appeared to be stands to put things on. One stood next to his chair and held an assortment of belongings.

From the room down the passage, he could hear the soft murmur of Cybelle's voice now as she spoke, and then another voice, too. It was another woman, and he remembered what she had said about communications over a long distance. It seemed unbelievable that she could talk to someone on another world from here. Still, it seemed commonplace to her—and also to Dixon. That meant it was something he should just accept.

After a while he started to worry about the horses. It was clear that they would be staying here. If Cybelle was right, there was no way to leave until help came from her agency. The horses were still saddled and waiting outside—untended—and guilt began to nag at him. He needed to take care of them before morning. Everything was quiet now, but daylight could bring trouble.

He got up, shifted to look down the hallway again. Cybelle was still murmuring to the glimmer of light. He crossed to the door, opened it and slipped out. He was concerned that it would latch behind him and he wouldn't be able to get back in, so he left it ajar.

The security lights in the yard were bright enough that he couldn't see the stars, but the last moon was clear enough. It was traveling down the sky toward sunrise. The bay nickered at him, as if hoping for feed, and he patted the horse on the shoulder reassuringly, went to work.

He unsaddled both of them and rubbed them down with the saddle blankets—moving quickly through the ease of long practice. He slipped the bits and left them tethered to the rail—ignoring the mare's efforts to nip at him. He wished for a tree and a patch of grass, but the ground was bare in the yard. There was a little overhang that would provide shade during the day, but nothing better than that. He measured out grain for each of them, and then hefted one of the saddles and packs, headed toward the steps.

He stopped then. Dixon was waiting on the top step. He still had on the white shirt, but he had put on longer pants and shoes.

"Oh," the man said. "I heard you go out."

Ta Nyahl dropped his eyes automatically. The introduction had been odd, only a brief exchange of names—but he was used to Cybelle's direct ways by now. He tested the man's scent, found he seemed concerned, but not unfriendly.

Ta Nyahl decided to be bold. He moved toward the steps, and Dixon backed up to let him enter. He bent, dropped the tack beside the doorway.

"The horses," he said quietly.

"Oh," the man said, "yes."

"Is there a place to put them?" Ta Nyahl asked.

"A stable," Dixon said. He took a long breath, let it out. "You're right. They need to be put away. I'll take them to where they're supposed to go."

They both went out, and Ta Nyahl lifted the other saddle and pack, carried it into the building. The man Dixon was back from the stable in a few minutes. Ta Nyahl had shut the door, but apparently Dixon knew the security code. He didn't have any trouble getting back in. He sat down in one of the other chairs.

"So," he said. "Cybelle says you're a…kria?"

The sound flowed very poorly over his tongue, but the word was understandable.

"Yes," said Ta Nyahl.

It seemed very strange to sit and talk this way with a human man. It had taken him a long time to get used to Cybelle. That had been forced on him, but now he found it wasn't so hard to be in this man's presence. He was careful to keep his eyes downcast, though, and not to look at Dixon directly. It wouldn't do to have problems with him.

"And…you live over the mountains?"

"Yes," said Ta Nyahl again. "In the forest."

"How did you run into Cybelle?"

Ta Nyahl felt his face begin to burn. He was still filled with shame for his failures—but it wouldn't show in the dimness of the room. He struggled with it, twisting a bit of leather trim between his fingers.

"It's not a good tale," he said finally.

"What happened to her face?" asked Dixon. "I can see the bruises even in this light."

He considered, couldn't see any reason to avoid the question. It was very direct, but the man likely had reason to be concerned about her.

"One of the villagers," he said.

"Yours?" asked Dixon.

"No," he said, "it wasn't kria who did that." He didn't mean to explain that the men who were responsible for it were dead. He would leave that for Cybelle. "It has been a hard trip to get here," he said.

"I can see that," said Dixon. "Do you…"

But Cybelle interrupted what else he might have wanted to ask. She appeared in the passageway.

"Ta Nyahl," she said. "Could you come, please?"

He got up, moved past the man Dixon and followed her up the passageway into the room with the equipment.

"Sit here in front of the display," she said, pointing out a chair in front of the witch light.

He eased into it, not sure of what to do.

"This is Anita Kallik, a legal analyst at the Commerce Agency," said Cybelle. "She's going to handle the things you want done."

He found the display featured a woman's face. She looked older than Cybelle, with a broad face and pale hair bound into a knot on top of her head.

The woman gasped and her mouth dropped open as he sat down. It was clear that she could see him, the blue-gray mask and the yellow eyes must have been clear even in the dim light of the room. He dropped his gaze in response, surprised that the woman seemed so close and real. Cybelle moved, and he thought she was going to leave him. He looked up.

"Don't go…" he said, suddenly desperate.

"I won't," she said. "I'm just going to pull up another chair. Anita will ask you questions, and you just answer. I'll be right here if you don't understand something."

It sounded so kindly that he almost thought it was unlike her. He glanced back at the display. The woman Anita seemed to have composed herself.

"Ahh," she said. "I'm ready to take your complaint first. The system will record what you say, so please just answer the questions. Do you understand?"

"Yes," he said.

"What is your name?"

He looked at Cybelle.

"Your full name," she said. "Is there more to it? Something more formal?"

"Ta Nyahl of clan Waxing Moon, son of Ta Marnie," he said, as if he were introducing himself to a kria. He said it in his own language, but when Anita looked blank, he said it again in the human's language. "Ta Nyahl of clan Waxing Moon."

"Oh," she said. "Alright. And you have a complaint about…genocide?"

He knew the word.

"Yes," he said.

"Against whom?" she asked.

He grappled with the question.

"The humans here," he said finally. "The people of Waxing Moon clan are all dead, except for me. They were killed by raiders from the Tanner village, and I heard the humans there say they would receive a bounty for dead kria."

"How many people were killed?"

"One hundred and twenty one in Waxing Moon clan," he said. "But other of the kria camps are also at risk. They are hidden from the human men in the forest valley across the mountains from here. Many others have died, as well."

"Alright," she said. "How do you know this about deaths in the Waxing Moon clan?"

"My cousins and I went out to hunt in the morning from the camp of our people, and when we returned, all were dead. We followed the raiders back to the Tanner village."

"You saw them in the camp?"

"Yes," he said.

"Did you see them kill anyone?"

"Not there," he said. "But I did see them disfigure the bodies of my kin. They laughed and talked about how they had killed everyone in the camp. Later I saw them kill my cousin Da Kathan and torture my cousin Da Hanath to death."

"Torture?" she said. "Do you have proof of this?"

He searched for what she meant.

"Yes," he said. "Cybelle Lawton saw this, too."

"Show her your arms," said Cybelle.

He looked at her, realized she meant the still healing burn scars. He got up from the chair and took off the leather jacket, rolled up the sleeves of the woolen shirt to show them to Anita. He lifted the hem of the shirt, too, showed her the marks on his sides and belly.

"Anita," said Cybelle, "I can verify that he got these at the Tanner village. I was there."

"Okay," Anita said. "That's good enough. I've got it recorded. So," she went on. "Are the kria at war with humans there?"

"The kria do not make war the way humans do," he said. "My people try to avoid trouble. The humans torture their own people, too."

"Human rights abuses, too?" she asked. "Ahhh. So who's offering the bounty?"

"I'm sorry?" he asked.

Cybelle leaned in toward the display. "We don't know, Anita. Have you got my report there about the Berlman Company application? There's possible motive there."

"Yes," said Anita. "I've got it linked. So Ta Nyahl," she said, "do you want to request an investigation to find out who's responsible?"

"An investigation?" he repeated. "What is that?"

"Someone to come and find out who is behind the bounty," she said.

"Yes," he said. "I want to know. And I want the genocide to stop."

Anita looked at him across the distance. Her face seemed very sober.

"We'll take care of it," she said.

Cybelle leaned in again. "Send us a good-sized security force, too, Anita. I'm really concerned about our safety here."

"Will do," said Anita. She frowned, looking unhappy. "I'll get someone out as soon as I can, Cybelle. Do you think you'll be safe for a day or so?"

"I don't know," said Cybelle. She rubbed her hands together, sounding worried. "There's a lot at stake here, Anita. We'll do what we can."

"So now," said Anita. "Ta Nyahl, Cybelle says you want to file a claim through adverse possession?"

He wasn't sure he followed that, but he glanced at Cybelle, saw in her face that this was what he wanted.

"Yes," he said, "for the kria. The human company means to destroy this world, and my people need it to live on."

"How long have the kria been there?" asked Anita.

It was the same questions Cybelle had asked, so he had the answers ready. It seemed to take a long time. After a while, he became aware of the room lightening, of objects taking shape around them as light came through the clear panes set in the walls. When they were done, the rosy colors of dawn were brightening the yard outside.

The image of Anita Kallik winked out, and Cybelle leaned across and touched a plate. Lighted symbols flowed. The witch light screen went out, too.

"Let's get something to eat," said Cybelle, "and then we can sleep for a while."

When they went back down the passage, he could see the man Dixon was cooking breakfast. There wasn't any open fire, but the skillet was obvious. It was only one more thing to accept.

The breakfast was warm in his stomach and filling, even though the food was strange. They sat in chairs around what Cybelle said was a table to eat, and he thought Dixon tried not stare at him too openly. It was enough to be uncomfortable, regardless.

When they were done, Cybelle pushed back her chair.

"Dixon," she said. "Thank you so much. I'll clean up here if you'll show Ta Nyahl how to use the plumbing. Do you have a change of clothes he could wear? And could you show him one of the bedrooms? I need to sleep myself—I am totally exhausted—but we need to talk first. Okay?"

Ta Nyahl got a quick lesson in how to make water run in one of the rooms, something like a waterfall that was warm and relaxing. When he was finished bathing, he found that Dixon had left pants and a soft shirt like he was wearing that fit fairly well. He put them on and lay on the soft pallet that the man had called a bed. Like Cybelle, he was exhausted, but he didn't fall into sleep right away. He lay and stared at a pale-colored ceiling.

Oddly, he felt empty now that the business with the agency was done. Both Cybelle and the women Anita has seemed bent on stopping the destruction of the world, but just now he wondered if the kria weren't already lost. It seemed so unlikely that someone as far away as Anita—who looked like a ghost on the screen—could do anything about what was happening here. It seemed like he had fallen into unreality somehow.

But really they were only waiting. Everything they had been working toward was done, and now they could only wait for the result. If what Cybelle had said was right, someone should be realizing soon that they had come in through the gate during the night, and were here now. Everything seemed quiet outside—but it was still early. Here and there were sounds of people stirring, but no one came to the building. Cybelle was right that they needed to get some sleep. Still, sleeping in the camp of the enemy was dangerous business. Just in case there was trouble, he got up and placed his boots and his weapons close beside the bed. Then he lay down again, feeling a little better prepared for trouble.

It seemed Cybelle had used the shower the same way he had. He heard her come out of her room and walk down the passage, and she and Dixon sat down at the table where they had eaten breakfast. It was a little distance away, but not so far that he couldn't hear what they said. The words carried well enough up the hallway.

"So," said Dixon. "What happened to your face?"

"I got captured by two hunters," she said. "From the Dirkin village, I think. They beat me up and tried to rape me. I shot one of them and…Ta Nyahl took care of the other."

"That boy?" he said. "He doesn't look like he'd hurt a flea."

"He's tough as nails," she said, "and very capable. He got me here. I've…I was scared of him for a while. You should take him seriously, Dixon."

"Why is he so shy?" he asked.

"I don't know if it's a species thing or not," she said. "It probably is. Did you notice the fangs? He's a carnivore, so I gather he's making a serious effort to be low-key and non-threatening."

"Fangs?" he said.

"You didn't notice?"

"No," he said. "I guess I should be more observant—so what happened to the men who attacked you?"

"They're both dead," she said. "It's something else I'll have to deal with."

"Dead," he repeated. "You killed one of the villagers?"

"When you've got a minute, read what I sent in my report," she said. "This colony is supposed to be maintained, but it's fallen into savagery. The conditions are primitive, and the colonists are out of control as far as human rights go. They practice war, slavery, torture, witchcraft, rape and apparently genocide against the kria. There should have been some kind of interference a long time ago."

"It's on the Berlman Company," he said. "They contracted for the colonists, and supporting the culture is their responsibility."

"So what's the problem?" she asked. "They've not sent anyone out here in a long time?"

"Probably not," he said. "The mining operations are automated, and there's not much need for maintenance.

They must not have realized the kria where here until after they submitted the plan for the destructive mining. Right?"

"That makes sense," she said. "It was probably something the corporate office cooked up. They submitted it, and then they sent somebody out here to make sure it went off as planned. So, Marx is the manager. He would have been the man in the crosshairs. Do you think he's behind the bounty?"

There was silence while he thought about it.

"Very likely," he said. "It would be his responsibility to make sure everything matched up to the application. It's possible the directive about a bounty came from the corporate office, but I just can't see it. If Marx and his team sent the information in, then he's trying to clean up his mistakes."

Cybelle's breath went out—an audible sigh.

"Dixon," she said. "I need to apologize to you. There's going to be trouble over this, and I've caught you in it."

"Ahhh," he said. "If I'd known, I could have left last week. But I didn't know you were coming." It sounded wry.

"Have you got a weapon?" she asked.

"Dammit," he said. "You think things will come to that?"

"Dixon, I do," she said. "There's a lot at stake here."

"Thanks for the warning," he said.

"I hope you won't need it," she said. "But it's best to be prepared." The chair she was sitting in creaked as she leaned back in it. "God, I'm exhausted," she said.

"Have you been up all night?" he asked. "Don't you need to get some rest?"

"Yes," she admitted. "You're right. I'm completely on edge, but I'll see if I can't sleep a while."

The chairs moved, and then silence fell.

Chapter 15

Ta Nyahl dreamed he was searching for the base. He was riding the gray mare through a desolate landscape, and Cybelle was with him. A heavy darkness lay all around, and he felt a desperate need to find the base, so she could do something about all the things that were wrong. The night was passing quickly, and he knew they had to get there before daylight. He kept seeing the lights of the yard, but as he approached, they only shifted and moved further away.

He turned in the saddle to tell Cybelle that something was wrong, that sorcery must be at work to move the lights that way, but she was gone from behind him. When he looked back at the base, it was on fire. It looked the same way the Tanner village had when he and his cousins had fired the palisade. He sat on the horse and watched as the hungry flames leaped from one building to the next like contagion, thinking it was his chances to win this battle going up with the dark column of smoke above. He moved in his sleep, wishing he could…

He snapped awake. There had been a sound at the door in the front room.

Dixon had been moving around the space in the front of the building, but Ta Nyahl knew he was there—it hadn't disturbed his sleep. This was something different, though, and he felt a stab of panic—an adrenaline rush that set his heart to beating hard. Someone from outside had come to the door. He heard Dixon walk toward it, open the panel.

"Dieter Marx," he said from the other room. "How's it going?"

"Morning, Thomas," said a man's voice. "Renny told me Ms. Lawton is back this morning."

"Yeah," said Dixon. "She did come in during the night."

"I thought I'd drop by and see if she was alright," said Marx. "Can I come in?"

"Sure," said Dixon. "She's sleeping right now."

The man's steps entered the room.

"Is she alright?"

"A little the worse for wear," said Dixon, "but I don't think she needs medical attention, if that's what you mean. She seems to be fine."

Ta Nyahl moved cautiously, rolled off the bed. His weapons were there if he needed them, but he didn't mean for the man to see him. He felt an urge to escape, to get out of the confined quarters of the room into more open space. He looked at the window, knowing that it opened, but he couldn't see how it worked. He would have to find out. He looked out the pane set in it, found the yard seemed clear outside. His heart was still beating hard—but there didn't seem to be any immediate threat. He hesitated. That meant the best choice was stillness and waiting. He moved on silent feet, crouched against the wall by the doorway.

The door was open a small space. Looking through it, he could see that Dixon and the man Marx were standing just inside the doorway. Marx was tall and dark-haired, with big shoulders, sharp-cut features and thick eyebrows.

"Did she come in by herself?" he asked Dixon.

The two saddles were still lying on the floor by the doorway—it would be clear that she hadn't.

"No," said Dixon. "As a matter of fact, she brought someone with her. A guide, I think she said, from over the mountains."

Dixon was very cool and composed, and Ta Nyahl thought he had a warrior's nerve. This was the man Dixon and Cybelle has said might be behind the bounty. Plus, Cybelle thought they might be in danger here—from this man, most likely. Still, there was no sign of it in Dixon's voice.

"Sit down," he said. "Do you want a cup of coffee?"

"Sure," said Marx. "Cream and sugar."

Dixon made rummaging noises, and then Ta Nyahl heard liquid pour, smelled the strong scent of the brew. The man brought back two cups, gave one to Marx. He sat down in another of the chairs.

Just then Cybelle's door opened, and she came out of her room. Of course, the noise would have wakened her, too. She was dressed in a soft shirt and long pants similar to Dixon's. She moved down the passageway, clipping up her hair.

"Good morning, Mr. Marx," she said. "I'm awake. I've slept well."

The scents were starting to work their way up the passageway now. Of course the humans wouldn't be aware of them. They all stank of fear and anger and desperation—but there was nothing of it in their voices.

"There you are," said Dixon. "Do you want some coffee, Cybelle?"

"Sure," she said.

The coffee had a heady smell, very pleasant, but still it couldn't mask the storm of emotions. Apparently nothing would come of it at this meeting, though. Perhaps Marx had only come to scout out the situation. Ta Nyahl eased down to a sitting position against the wall, settled in to listen to them talk.

"What happened to your face?" asked Marx.

"Just a little accident in the woods," said Cybelle. The bruises were lightening now and starting to fade, but they were still dark and ugly. "I'm alright."

"I'm so glad you're back safely," said Marx. "We hadn't given up on the search, but at this point, I had very little confidence we could find you. What happened? Did you get lost from the flyer?"

"Circumstances beyond my control," she said. "I'm really sorry if I've caused you any trouble. I did find a guide to bring me back here."

It sounded like fencing, as if the man Marx wanted information that he didn't want to ask, and Cybelle said things that didn't tell him anything. It would never have worked among the kria, who could read the signs of lying in the scent. Everyone was lying here, he thought. The smell of it filled the rooms.

"I suppose you'll get back to work then?" asked Marx. "Or have you finished up your survey?"

"I think we're about done with it," said Cybelle. "Dixon, is that right?"

"Ah, yes," said Dixon. "I'm done with my part of it."

"I've gotten a little behind, myself," said Cybelle, "but we should wind it up soon." She actually managed to smile coolly at the man, as if nothing at all were wrong.

Ta Nyahl thought they were talking about their investigation of the application. They were done with that already, he thought. Cybelle had sent in her report this morning before sunrise. They just weren't letting Marx know it.

"We'll have to call and set up passage home this week," said Cybelle. "Thank you for your hospitality."

Ta Nyahl could feel her anger behind that, but nothing of it showed in her face. Her smile could be very sweet when she wanted it to seem that way.

Marx looked at her doubtfully. He must wonder if she had really made the trip through the forest valley and across the mountains and not seen or heard anything damning. He looked at the saddles lying in the floor.

Ta Nyahl was the problem, of course. Marx must know she had brought a kria onto the base with her. If the camera at the gate hadn't been clear enough, the headmen at the villages would have let them know who she was traveling with.

"Well," said Marx. He got to his feet, apparently resigned to getting no information from her. "I'll be getting along then. I just wanted to make sure you were okay."

"Thanks for your concern," she said. "That's very kind of you."

Marx took one last look at the tack before he went out the door.

"Damn," said Cybelle. "I can't believe he came in here like that."

"He does have some brass," said Dixon.

"I wish I knew what he was thinking," she said. "Did you pick anything up?"

"No," said Dixon.

Ta Nyahl pushed up to his feet, slipped out the door of his room and into the passageway.

"He is full of fear," he said.

Their heads turned that way.

"How can you tell?" asked Cybelle, but then she thought. "Oh," she said. "He smells of it?"

He made sure there was no one at the windows. Everything seemed clear, so he stepped out into the room and stopped at the seat Marx had left. His scent still clung to it, a sharp tang of panic.

"Yes," he said. "You think this is the man who offered the bounty?"

"Did you hear that last night?" said Cybelle. "We're only guessing."

"But the agency's investigation will find out?"

"I hope so," she said. "They generally do a good job."

He thought about it, measuring what she said against what the man had felt when he saw her. That much fear had to have some cause. It suggested that she and Dixon had been right in their assessment of how the company had sent the man Marx to make sure the application was approved. He would have been responsible for making the world look like the application said it was. That meant he was likely in fear of what would happen if he failed.

"Well," said Cybelle. She moved to stand up. "While we're not doing anything, let me show you how the kitchen works."

She got up and showed him where they stored food and dishes, and how the water and the cooking stove worked. The arrangement seemed very foreign. He had already decided to accept things as he found them, though, and just tried to memorize how it went.

Cybelle got supplies from the refrigerator and made a lunch of cheese and very fine, soft bread. Ta Nyahl tried some of the coffee and found it tasted very bad, regardless that it smelled good. He poured it down the sink and got plain water to drink instead.

After they had eaten and cleaned up the dishes, there seemed nothing else to do. Dixon paced, stopping now and then to look out the windows. Apparently there wasn't much to see, either—only the buildings and the fence.

"Can't you sit down?" asked Cybelle, finally. "You're driving me crazy—and they'll see you staring out the widows."

He sat down, but in a few minutes he was back to pacing again. About mid-afternoon his vigilance paid off.

"There are flyers coming in," he said.

Cybelle got up from where she had been sitting in one of the chairs and leaned over to look alongside him. Ta Nyahl got up, too, shifted so he could see what they were talking about.

It did look like what he had seen from the mountain. There were two of them. They had something like a bird shape, and they were glassy and dark. They settled slowly on a cushion of air onto a field out near the gate where they had come through last night. Once the flyers had stopped, hatches opened in the sides and human men climbed down.

"It looks like your search party from the forest," said Dixon.

Ta Nyahl thought he meant it was the men they had spent so much effort to escape in the woods. Someone from here must have called them back, let them know that Cybelle had slipped past them and gotten to the base on her own. They would have left their horses and tack behind in one of the villages, taken the flyers to soar over the mountains and back to the base. It was clear that the flyers were very fast. In only one day, they had come the distance it had taken Cybelle and Ta Nyahl a cycle of the smallest moon to cover.

"Ah," said Cybelle. "I'm not sure I like that."

He understood what she meant. Marx may have had only a handful of men here at the base when they came, but now he had a larger force. There was nothing to do about it, though. Someone went out to meet the men from the furthermost building—not Marx, but someone else with a lighter build. The men shouldered packs of their belongings and carried them to what must be their living quarters in the buildings nearer that side of the compound.

A little while after that, Dixon started to get out supplies to make an evening meal. After they had eaten, he started to pace again. Ta Nyahl would have liked to do the same. He felt confined in the building—but for now he thought they would be safer inside here than outside. The night might be something different, though. He felt a quiver along his nerves, but there was nothing to do about it now. With the patience of a kria, he sat quietly on the floor and worked on repairing a strap for one of the saddlebags.

When dusk started to fall, the security lights winked on outside. Cybelle got up and started to pull down shades over the windows.

"They'll be able to see us when we turn the lights on," she explained.

Dixon had stopped pacing, but he still looked at the windows nervously. The darkness meant they needed to make plans for sleeping.

"Lhassa," asked Ta Nyahl. "Should we set a watch for the night?"

Cybelle raised her brows at Dixon.

"Do you think it would help?" she asked.

"Surely you don't think he would attack us here," said Dixon. The idea upset him.

"Why not?" she asked. "I wouldn't have thought they'd attack me on a survey outing, but they did."

"What would be the point?" he asked.

"If we just disappeared," she said, "they could challenge my report and start over with a new assessment team."

He looked at her blankly.

"Dixon," she said. "There's a lot of money at stake here."

He rubbed at his face. It was clear that the stress was wearing on him. Like most humans, he hadn't the endurance of the kria, who could wait out a siege in relative serenity.

"I think we need to do it," she said. "How should we go about it?"

He frowned.

"If I thought it would work," he said, "I'd be happy to sit here all night. Do you want to set a sentry outside?"

She frowned, ran her long fingers through the strands of her hair.

"No," she said. She glanced at Ta Nyahl, shook her head. "It's too big a risk. I think we all need to stay inside."

"You can't see crap from in here," Dixon said. "Out front in the yard, yes—but everything behind the building is completely dark."

"So we're just sitting ducks until morning, regardless?" she asked.

"I'd say that's it," he said.

"I think I'll sleep in my clothes," she said.

"And keep your weapon under the pillow," he said. "I changed the security code on the door again this afternoon."

"Well, that's good," she said. "At least they'll have to break the door down to get at us."

He laughed, a short, ugly bark of mirth. "It should keep them busy for all of thirty seconds."

She didn't seem to think it was funny.

"Well," she said. "I'm still pretty exhausted. Do you mind if I take the first watch? Then I can have uninterrupted sleep for a while."

"It's fine with me," he said.

"Will you take the second?" she asked. "And then Ta Nyahl can take the third and get us through until daylight. I'm sure he's tired, too."

Since they had decided, Dixon went on to bed—but not before Ta Nyahl asked him how to open the windows.

He went to the room they had given him and lay on the bed. He would have liked to stay awake, but like Cybelle, he felt the effects of recent exhaustion—he needed to sleep. Still, he lay awake for a while, listening for sounds outside.

This wasn't an easy position to defend. Dixon was right that they couldn't see anything from inside the building. The yard in front was well lighted, but dark shadows clothed the back and far side of it toward the fence. Ta Nyahl had managed to get the window open so the night air came in, bringing sounds and scents along with it. He doubted the little opening would help him sense anything like an attack before it happened, but it made the room seem less confining. He made sure his weapons were ready. After a while he dropped into a fitful sleep.

Chapter 16

He was choking.

Dixon's shout had wakened him, he thought. He coughed, rolled out of the bed. The air was thick and heavy with smoke—the building was on fire. The men had fired it. Of course, they should have expected it.

It was sometime in the dead of night, and the room was already filled with heat and eddies of smoke. The air was better near the floor—good enough that he could breathe in short gasps. He panted, pulled on his boots, felt for the bow and quivers he had left by the bed. He moved across the room to open the door, found it was hot. It was a warning, so he only pulled it open a small space.

Heat struck him like a blow—the fire was raging on the other side. He shut the door again quickly. He crossed the room, raised his eyes carefully over the windowsill, looked out. The space outside was pitchy dark, flaring with shadows from the flame. He waited for his eyes to adjust, saw nothing but the fence a little distance away. He reached for Ka Tehnie's ivory pin on the bed table, caught it in his teeth. Then he grabbed for his leather jacket and went out the window.

It was a small opening. He wouldn't have been able to do it with the jacket on. Without it, his shoulders were flexible enough that he could fit them through the small rectangle, slide out on the other side. The fire was nearly on him. He dropped to the ground, jerked up and ran to get clear—he had to smother another fit of coughing then. His eyes watered, burning from the smoke and fumes.

What he had thought from the room seemed right. There was no one waiting in the darkness behind the building. His head cleared in the better air, and his breathing eased. He put on the jacket quickly, hoping it would give him some protection—at least it was dark-colored. He slung the quivers over his shoulder and stung his bow.

It seemed there would be a battle. He looked both ways along the fence, saw nothing yet. Scent was useless to him—all he could smell was the fire. All he could hear was the roar from the flames. It didn't matter. As he walked along the back of the building, he braided up his hair, set the ivory pin in it. He didn't need it to be flying in his face.

The second moon had just risen, and the security lights were out in the yard. Still, the fire was bright enough to light it. It bellowed like an angry demon, the hungry flames licking at the walls. The men had fired the building with piles of brush along the sides of the structure. That meant they had caught Cybelle and Dixon inside—they couldn't have gotten out the windows further back.

How many men were there? He made a quick count of those he had seen. Twelve from the flyers, and at least two more that had been here. Fourteen? Sixteen? He could expect they were waiting somewhere in the yard to see what the effects of the fire would be.

There were six buildings in the compound. The main one was larger and set against the fence on the other side of the yard from where he was. To the left of it was a smaller structure. Three other small building lay on this side of yard, roughly facing the others. The building he had been sleeping in lay behind those, nearly against the fence. The two flyers sat on their flat field near the gate.

The men must have been fairly confident that they had caught everyone inside the building. Otherwise, they would have had someone guarding the back of it. Still—perhaps not. The heat from the fire was intense. They might be staying well back for safety reasons. Ta Nyahl set off walking, made a careful circle around the burning back corner. He stayed close to the fence, feeling the buffet of heated wind from the flames. From the point where he stopped, he could easily see along the front side of the building.

If Cybelle and Dixon were still alive, they had to be in the front of the structure, right at the door. The men would be waiting for them to come out.

That seemed to be right. He crouched in the shadows, shielded his eyes with both hands against the bright glow of the flames. The human men were grouped around the next building toward the yard, well out of the light and watching the door.

As he identified them, he saw the door to the burning building open. There was a sharp crack, and splinters flew from the side of the building—a shot from some kind of weapon. The door slammed shut.

So, they meant to keep Cybelle and Dixon inside until the fire was done with them. If he could help at all, he needed to find shelter somewhere else—the fire made this a very bad place to be. He looked for cover further out in the yard, located something that might be a well housing in the flickering darkness. He darted toward it, ducked into the shadow.

He heard something break, saw it was Dixon who was beating a pane out to let air in. Splinters jumped from the wall next to the window—another shot. The man ducked backward.

Ta Nyahl had seen where the shot came from this time. The weapon they used had made a spark of fire as the report sounded. He reached backward, pulled an arrow out of his quiver. He drew the bow, let the arrow fly before the man could move.

It must have struck true. There was a shout from the men and the mass of them shifted suddenly in the darkness. They had realized he was there. He sent off another shot, saw their shadows dodge behind the building. They dragged at least one man who had fallen.

He nocked another arrow. The door opened a crack, and he saw Cybelle peer out. They must have seen the men withdraw from inside. When there was no shot in response, she jerked the door open and jumped down the steps, ran for the building on her left. Dixon leaped down the steps, too, ran behind her.

It was a risky thing to do. Only the fact that they would die otherwise made it a good choice. Dirt flew up at their feet. Fire had blossomed from around the edge of the building. Ta Nyahl let his arrow fly. This time they knew where he was, though. Something spanged off the pipes in front of him, struck him in the shoulder.

It threw him backward. He landed heavily, took a breath, tried to decide how badly he was hit.

It wasn't like an arrow wound. Something small and deadly had struck him in the shoulder—his chest felt numb. Ta Nyahl managed to roll over. He made sure he was still under cover, checked to see what had happened.

The shot from the weapon must have hit the pipe and then gone into his chest. The bone plates on the jacket had shattered under the impact, but they had protected him some. The wound was bleeding, but it didn't seem to have broken his shoulder. He wouldn't die right away from it, but it would sap his strength.

It was starting to hurt now. He took a shaky breath, let it out. He had done what he needed to do. Cybelle and Dixon were safe from the fire—at least for now. The immediate problem was over, and he wasn't dead—yet.

He could faintly hear Cybelle and Dixon coughing now above the roar of the flames. He wondered briefly if they might somehow be able to stay clear until morning—but that wouldn't work, he could tell. The men who had been arrayed along the building in front of him shifted, rearranged their forces. Someone made a shot, and there was an answer from Cybelle's weapon. Fire lanced out from it like a shaft of light, left a glowing afterimage on his retinas. The shadows dodged backward.

While they were busy, he needed to find better cover—the well housing was hardly broad enough to hide behind. There was little choice of where to go. The only possibility was the building in front of him, but that would mean going to ground right in front of Marx' men. The band of them were behind it now, jockeying for a better position against Cybelle's weapon. He checked their location again—watched for a moment when they were all focused on her and Dixon. Then he pushed up, made a limping run across the open space.

It seemed no one noticed. He dropped, rolled under the building. He worked his way further under, well away from unfriendly eyes. Then he laid his face down against the gritty soil, trying to control his breath in the cool darkness. His shoulder burned with a fiery ache now, and he felt dizzy and sick. He must have left a blood trail; they would find him easily enough in daylight. Still, the darkness was a cover for now.

Cybelle and Dixon had barely gotten out of the burning building in time. Across from him, it was completely enveloped in flame. The fire roared and crackled like some hungry animal as it devoured the timbers, consumed the walls. He could see the fiery skeleton of the rafters glowing through it now. In a few moments more, the roof would fall in.

Ta Nyahl closed his eyes against the flames, feeling a pain that was more than just physical. It seemed the worst that Cybelle had predicted would come true—they were all going to die. He would liked to have protected her. He would liked to have lived long enough to know the petition he gave to Anita Kallik had worked, and that this world might belong to the kria someday. It seemed very massive and enduring as he lay on it, but he knew now that it was as tenuous as his own life, only a spot in the field of stars that could be here at this moment and gone in an instant the next.

He opened his eyes then, realized that was close enough to the human men that he could hear them talk. He could hear the sound of their boots as they moved.

"What happened to the damn kria?" asked one of them.

He thought it was Marx. Would the man be here directing the strategy?

"Wasn't he inside the building?" answered another.

"It was an arrow that brought down Hendrix," said Marx. "He got out—the bastard is out here somewhere."

"Messer got him," said a third voice. "I saw him go down."

"Is Hendrix alright?" asked the second voice.

"Nah," said the third. "Jamison, he's a goner. The arrow shot was dead on."

It was nice to know the human men were one less. Ta Nyahl writhed inwardly, aching with the knowledge that he was helpless now—that he wouldn't be able to bring down any more of them. He wasn't sure now that he could even draw the bow. He felt a burning shame at his weakness, but there was little he could about it. He drew a long, slow breath and let it out, tried to get a grip on the pain and sickness. Lying with his head on the earth seemed to help.

"You're sure he went down?" asked Marx. "I don't want him sneaking up on us."

"Yeah," said another of them men. "The shot hit him. I saw him fall."

"Where?" asked Marx.

"Over by the well," said the man.

"I need his body when we're done tonight," said Marx. "We..."

Ta Nyahl heard the crunch of approaching boot steps.

"Marx," interrupted a voice he hadn't heard before. "You need to rethink what you're doing here."

The man sounded angry.

"Renny," said Marx, "we've been through this. As the assistant manager, you're as much responsible for this as I am."

Marx was annoyed. His voice snapped with cold arrogance.

"I don't agree with murder," said the man Renny.

"It's self-preservation," said Marx. "You know how ruthless company management is…"

"Self-interest isn't everything," said the man.

"So what are you going to do?" said Marx. "Resign right now? Renny, you're in this as deep as I am."

"Am I?" asked Renny.

"You are. You're either for me or against me, Renny. I can deal with you, too."

There was a moment of silence then, filled by the noise of the fire. It was a threat, and the man Renny knew it.

"Okay, Marx," he said finally. "You're the boss."

"I'm glad you understand that," said Marx. His tone was cold. "So, we need to get this under control," he said. "Get me those agency people. Take half the men and circle around behind them. They'll surrender once they see there's no other option. We'll look for the kria later."

"Yes, sir," said Renny. Clearly, he had submitted to Marx' authority as the manager. "Messer, Allenden, Wren, Keller, Jamison," he said, "come with me."

The plan seemed to work as Marx predicted—Ta Nyahl watched it play out from under the shelter of the building. The men with Marx fired shots to keep Cybelle and Dixon from realizing the other party was creeping up behind them. After a moment he heard Renny shout.

"Lawton and Thomas! You're surrounded. Drop your weapons!"

There was no exchange of weapons fire this time, so it was clear they had surrendered. After another few moments, he heard their footsteps crunch along the bare ground.

"Hello, Marx," said Cybelle.

"Miss Lawton," said Marx, "Mr. Thomas. I'm glad you decided to give up."

"Is it going to do us any good?" asked Dixon.

"I'm afraid not," said Marx.

The fire had died enough that he could hear Cybelle cough.

"Marx," she said. "It won't do any good to kill us. I already filed my report. I denied your application."

"My dear," he said. "I'm sure we could appeal. You just misunderstood the situation."

"I didn't," she said. "It will be clear enough—the agency knows the kria are here now."

"That won't matter," he said. "The kria have got nothing. There's no evidence to show they're not the treacherous savages we say they are."

"We're scheduled to be picked up," she said. "There will be someone here soon looking for us."

"Your deaths will be easy to explain," he said. "You brought one of those vicious kria in with you, and he turned on you. He killed you, set fire to the buildings. We did all we could, but we couldn't save you."

Ta Nyahl heard curses—a struggle, and then someone fell. It was Dixon, he thought. He could see the man's white shirt where he lay on the ground.

Every instinct said he should lie still and be quiet. He was hidden by the darkness. Once the fire went out, it might be possible scale the fence and escape into the wastelands.

His clothes were dark and invisible—no one had seen him slide into the space under the building. He was safe for the moment.

He didn't like what he was hearing, though. It sounded as if Marx would kill both of them and throw their bodies into the fire. Anita had seemed very sure that she could take care of any problems that came up with Cybelle's report and his claim on this world. But could she still do that once Cybelle was dead?

The question came down to Marx. From what Cybelle had said, his company must be very powerful. It traded in worlds, after all. This one was only so much dirt and rock to the men behind it. It seemed they would be willing to kill everyone here in order to get what they wanted. If they were that powerful, could Cybelle's agency really stop them?

The man sounded so arrogant, as if he were completely sure of himself. He had come to talk to Cybelle in the morning, and he had called his men back from the forest. Then he had made up this plan to kill them all so he could start over with his application. And the worst of it was, he meant to blame the kria for an attack on his base and the death of Cybelle and Dixon. That was a problem of honor— and Ta Nyahl had sworn an oath to this woman, even if it took his life to serve her.

The question now was whether he could really lie here still and quiet, let Cybelle and Dixon die, and maybe manage to escape in the darkness before dawn—or if he needed to do something to stop this. There was no one else to ask about it, no elders to give him council. This was the man who had likely killed his kin—his mother, his father, his brother— his cousins. This was the man who had offered a bounty for dead kria, who had encouraged the torture and death of Da Hanath and Da Kathan. Ta Nyahl whispered a brief prayer to his predecessors, but he already knew the answer. He was Waxing Moon's last warrior, and now he remembered his hatred of the men who had killed his kin. It rose up and filled him with calm—and a kind of peace.

His pain and sickness had quieted as he lay listening to them. Now he thought he might almost be able to achieve something like silent movement. He took a breath and shifted—found his body responded to the need. He eased forward—feeling his pain as something remote and distant—working away from the voices toward the opposite edge of the building.

From the crawlspace it was hard to see where they were. Still, he thought they were all on the side away from the fire—they had been grouped in the shadow where Cybelle and Dixon couldn't see to shoot at them. Now they had likely moved to surround Cybelle and Marx where they argued at the lighted end of the building. He rolled out from under the structure at the opposite end, carefully pushed up and leaned his back against the wall. It wasn't as hard as he had thought it might be. He felt light and free—his mind clear. There was more strength in his knees than he expected, and his hands were nearly steady.

The moon was setting. The shadows flowed like a river across the yard, wild and unworldly. He had a man's stature, and in the darkness, he could pass for one—at least for a while. The quivers would give him away, though— he couldn't carry those. He took out five arrows and stuck them into the waistband of his pants. The bow was harder to conceal—all he could do was close the jacket over it.

He checked, made sure his knife was ready in its case. He whispered another prayer, then he stepped casually around the corner of the building, glanced toward the group of men. No one was looking in his direction. They were all focused on Marx and Cybelle. Dixon lay on the ground, his white shirt dirtied by soot. There was no sign of blood on it—he must be only unconscious.

Ta Nyahl brushed one hand along the wall to steady himself, walked toward them. The men were slightly separated into two groups. The ones who had gone with Renny still stood in the open space between buildings, easy to see in the rushing firelight. Marx and the men who had stayed with him were standing in the shadow of this building. They were harder to identify, but his eyes were adjusted to the darkness. The fading moon wasn't bright in comparison to the fire, but its light was good enough that he could pick out Cybelle with her longer hair—and the man Marx.

Cybelle was complaining about the genocide. She sounded angry.

"I don't know what you were thinking to offer a bounty," she said. "You know the SIA will be here to investigate."

"There's nothing to investigate," said Marx. "I don't know where you heard all this, but it's not correct in any way."

The men were between him and Marx. Ta Nyahl took a breath. He pushed away from the wall, moved out into the open space so he could work around them. He caught his balance, moved easily. One of the men looked at him, apparently saw nothing out of the ordinary. It was as if his predecessors came to his aid when he needed them. His sight was clear, his hands were steady. The pain in his shoulder felt very distant. He focused, taking in of the flow of words.

"You can deny it all you want," Cybelle said, "but it's going to come back to you. Even if you deny personal responsibility, it's happened on your watch."

"The problem is," said Marx, "they'll never find the kria camps. There aren't that many of them left, and they're scared to death of people. They can send a whole team of xenologists to beat the bushes, but they'll never find a single one."

"I found one easily enough," said Cybelle. "I need to tell you, Marx, he's put in a claim on this world through adverse possession."

"What?" said Marx.

It had taken him aback. Apparently it wasn't something he had considered.

"After I filed my report," said Cybelle, "I got one of the legal analysts at the agency to handle it for him."

The man cursed. That was good. Maybe it meant the claim would be successful, after all—that Anita might be able make it work even against the power of Marx' company.

"He'll be discredited," said Marx. "When we're done, he won't be here to fight it."

"You won't get away with it," said Cybelle.

"Yes, I will," he said. "And now, my dear, your time is up…"

He hefted his weapon.

"No," said Ta Nyahl in the human language. "Yours is."

His shadow might pass for a man, but his tongue wouldn't. Marx jerked around to face him, and he let an arrow fly in the same instant.

The wound was mortal this time—he could tell. It felt as if a giant fist crushed one whole side of his chest.

The blow hurled him backward. The ground came up hard against his back. He heard Cybelle scream something. The man Renny was shouting, too—yelling something at the men. Then they all seemed gone from where they had been.

Ta Nyahl felt nothing at first. Only his strength was gone, and quickly it got hard to breathe. He coughed, and his mouth filled up with blood. He rolled onto his belly, dragged himself toward deeper shadow, the cover of the crawlspace. He spat weakly, but it did little good. The blood continued to come.

He heard quick footsteps behind him, the humans, he thought vaguely, coming to finish what they had begun. Their voices echoed through the darkness, close now as they called to one another. He lay still, instinct quieting even his struggle for breath. It was the automatic response of the hunted kria, hurt and crawling away to die, so that ironically, even though he died, the hunter wouldn't have the satisfaction of a trophy in the end. But it wasn't that studied. It was only instinct, after all—and the death of reason. He must have left a trail a child could follow, bleeding as he was. Lying still would gain him nothing now. Better to court a quick death.

A shadow darkened the faint moonlight above him, and fabric brushed leather as someone knelt. His mind had hazed. He started suddenly at a touch on his boot, but the action was more intention than fact. He had no real strength to move.

"Renny!" the voice called beside him. "Here!"

And then someone familiar was there, tugging at him, lifting his head from the bloodstained dirt. The pain was coming now, crushing and deadly. Confused, he tried to flinch away from her, but she only held him tighter.

"Ta Nyahl," she said. "Do you hear me?"

Darkness had drifted over him at the effort to breathe, and with it the little strength he had left was fading. She shook him, feeling the slackness that was invading his body.

"Ta Nyahl," she insisted. "Look at me. Who am I?"

He couldn't keep his eyes focused, let them fall shut again. He tried to say her name, but he had no breath for it, only coughed in a brief spasm and brought up more blood.

"Renny!" she cried desperately. "Hurry it up! I need a medic!"

"She's on the way," said Renny—suddenly close by.

"We've got to fix this," said Cybelle. "Marx was right. We'll never find the kria without him."

"I'm sorry," said Renny. "I tried to stop it…"

"Ta Nyahl," said Cybelle, "hold on for a while longer. We've got medical people that can help you."

"No," he tried to say. It only brought more blood.

He had accepted his dying, and he thought she couldn't help him now. He was cold, knew it was death creeping up. She stroked back the ragged bangs of his hair with a warm hand, wiped the blood off his face. It all seemed very distant.

"Oh, I'm sorry," she said. "I should have remembered that damned death wish."

It didn't matter now. It was too late for anything more.

"Lhassa…" he said through the blood in his mouth. And then the darkness fell on him, and he was gone.

Epilogue

Ta Nyahl opened his eyes in a strange place. It wasn't what he thought the afterworld would look like. Instead, it looked like one of the humans' places. It stank with an antiseptic sweetness. The walls were a pale green and curtains hung down from the ceiling. There was a faint beeping sound. He turned his head slightly.

Cybelle Lawton was sleeping in a chair beside the bed. He had lost a day or so, he thought. The bruises on her face were green today and nearly faded. There were dark circles under her eyes. The chair didn't look very comfortable for sleeping.

When he tried to move one hand, he found he was tied to the bed.

She must have heard him move. She started awake.

"Oh," she said. "Thank God."

He took an exploratory breath, found it worked much better than he would ever have expected. He wasn't happy to be where he was, but he really hadn't the strength to worry about it just now. He took another careful breath.

"Am I a prisoner?" he asked. His voice sounded rusty and unused—hardly more than a whisper.

"No," she said. "Of course, not. The doctor was only afraid you'd wake up in a panic and try to pull the tubes out. Don't bother them, okay?"

There were at least two. One seemed to be pinned to the skin of his wrist and the other went into his chest.

"They're just temporary," she said. "The one in your chest is to keep your lungs clear until they heal."

It seemed only another thing to accept.

"Alright," he said.

She reached over and pulled the restraints loose so his hands were free. That was a good sign. He lifted one hand, touched the tube in his chest experimentally. It seemed to be made of metal and soft tubing, and it must be working well enough. His breath was easy and clear. It still hurt to talk, though.

"Where are we?" he asked.

She pushed back her hair.

"On a ship," she said. "The medical facility was better here than the one on the base."

He thought it must be very fine, to have brought him back from death this way.

"What happened to Marx?" he asked.

She frowned. "I'm sorry to say they managed to save him, too."

He closed his eyes, disappointed to have failed.

"Ta Nyahl," she said, "I need to say thank you again. He would have killed me and Dixon, both."

It was a point of concern as well as honor.

"Wouldn't it be better for the kria if he had died?"

She rubbed at her cheek, propped up her head with one elbow on the chair arm.

"I don't think it matters now," she said. "There are other issues that are more important. Ta Nyahl, are you feeling okay? I need to talk to you about some things."

He thought she must want to know if his mind was working. Like his breath, it seemed clear.

"I'm well enough," he said.

She looked at him, as if suspicious he might be hiding the truth from her. He must have passed inspection, though.

"Okay," she said. "The first thing is that the people from the agency are here. There's a team of xenologists that has come along to make official contact with the kria."

It took him a moment to sort through what she meant. Regardless that things seemed to be going well with the humans at the moment, he still had only Cybelle's assurance that the claim would work and that it would now be safe for the kria to live on this world. He was caught in circumstances that were dangerous and stressful, and he couldn't expose his people to any of that. It would still be a betrayal to give away any information on the camps.

"No. Lhassa," he said. "The elders would need to…"

"I know," she said. "I know. But listen, I think the team will be happy with just you for now. Plus, I want to get you out of here—I think it would be safer all around if you were somewhere else."

She hesitated, as if unsure quite what to say.

"Would you be willing to stay with me for a while? As a liaison? We'll go back to my world on the ship, and you can look after your claim in person."

He only stared at her.

"Is there a problem with that?" she asked. "You can make decisions for yourself, can't you? You don't have to ask the elders?"

"Leave here on the ship?" he repeated.

"Yes," she said.

The idea was a little shocking. By now he was used to the fact that people came from other worlds, but the notion of going himself had never occurred to him—what it might be like to travel to other places that might be very different from this one. But actually, she had said they were on a ship now. If he understood how the ships worked, that meant they had already left the world and were somewhere above it. And now she was asking him to go further.

Reality shifted around him, rearranged. What she suggested would mean leaving all his people here and going out alone. The thought was wrenching. His clan might be gone, but he was still attached to this world, born to the forests and the seasons—the blue of the sea. He still had kin here. He didn't want to leave it forever.

"Would I ever come back?" he asked.

"Of course," she said. "If you're an official liaison, then you can come back any time you want. Anita already said she could set it up for you."

It was like standing on the edge of a high cliff, with blue misty depths below full of unseen dangers—but wonders, too. All it took was the courage to step off.

He closed his eyes. At this point, could he trust what Cybelle said? There were all kinds of problems with the idea, but in a way it made sense. He couldn't live his life forever in fear, and this work could give him purpose, a reason to move forward with living. Ka Tehnie had given him both a blessing and a release along with the ivory pin, but it was up to him to grasp the opportunities. He needed to follow through on what he had started here, make sure it didn't go wrong somewhere along the line. He wasn't sure what a liaison was supposed to do, but probably he could figure it out.

"You don't have to answer right now," she said. "But will you think about it?"

"Alright," he said.

Cybelle let her breath out.

"Wonderful," she said. She scrubbed at her eyes. "I'm so glad you're alright. Now I can get some real sleep."

She got up to go, but before she left the room, she reached out and laid her hand on his, squeezed gently.

"Thank you for what you did," she said. "We're alive because of you."

He didn't flinch away. He was actually pleased at her touch. Somehow it seemed full of promise.

About the Author

Lela E. Buis is an award-winning artist and writer. She couldn't decide on a career, so ended up working as a waitress, a gas station attendant, an engineer at Kennedy Space Center and as a teacher of various subjects and levels. She began writing as a child and leans toward genre fiction, having published mainly science fiction and fantasy stories and poetry. When she's not painting or writing, she looks after a disabled cat and a couple of part time dogs.